A Path Unknown

Naina Nair

 Cedar books

Published by:
Cedar books

An Imprint of
Pustak Mahal®, Delhi

J-3/16, Daryaganj, New Delhi-110002
☎ 23276539, 23272783, 23272784 • *Fax:* 011-23260518
E-mail: info@pustakmahal.com • *Website:* www.pustakmahal.com

Sales Centre

■ 10-B, Netaji Subhash Marg, Daryaganj, New Delhi-110002
☎ 23268292, 23268293, 23279900 • *Fax:* 011-23280567
E-mail: rapidexdelhi@indiatimes.com

■ 6686, Khari Baoli, Delhi-110006
☎ 23944314, 23911979

Branches

Bengaluru: ☎ 080-22234025 • *Telefax:* 22240209
E-mail: pustak@airtelmail.in • pustak@sancharnet.in
Mumbai: ☎ 022-22010941, 022-22053387
E-mail: rapidex@bom5.vsnl.net.in
Patna: ☎ 0612-3294193 • *Telefax:* 0612-2302719
E-mail: rapidexptn@rediffmail.com
Hyderabad: *Telefax:* 040-24737290
E-mail: pustakmahalhyd@yahoo.co.in

ISBN 978-81-223-1279-9

Edition 2012

Printed at : Param Offsetters, Okhla, New Delhi-110020

To my darling daughter
Akshita
There are times...
When a mother neglects her daughter
When a mother is angry with her daughter
Scolds her or doesn't speak to her...
There are times...
When a daughter can decide to be difficult
Get irritated with her mother
Retaliate, rebel and throw tantrums
But in the long run a mother realizes that
A daughter is one who never leaves her side...
And a daughter realizes that
A mother is one who loves her all her life.

Acknowledgements

My mother and my in-laws for their blessings.

My hubby Ajit for his constant support and guidance.

My nine-year-old son Kartik for his positive comments on every story I write.

My sister Leena for helping me with the last minute editing.

Beena and Simran for their support. They understood my need for solitude when I was writing the novel and never phoned me lest they disturb my line of thoughts... Great friends! Thank you both for being there...

Foreword

Life is a journey... several paths lie ahead of us...

Which path to choose? Which way to go? Who chooses the path?

Does destiny choose our path, or does it make us choose our path?

Walk undeterred, trust your step, you are guided by your inner self...

Don't look at the paths ahead... Just look inside yourself and ask...

Is this the right path?

You will get the answer... you will see the path... clearer than ever...

Chapter 1

Amartya stared at the beautiful girl sitting opposite her. *Something was terribly wrong with the girl who was so alive and yet looked so dead.* Amartya picked up the case file lying on the desk and opened it.

Patient Name: Shivani Ghose, age 25.

"Hello Shivani, I am Dr. Amartya John, your psychiatrist. How are you?"

She hoped she would get an answer. But Shivani's face was blank and her eyes stared into space. Who had done this to the poor girl? Dr. Amartya sighed. Shivani was her responsibility now. She would start treatment on the girl and bring back life in those lifeless eyes. Shivani had to become normal again. She had been admitted in a case of suicidal depression. Amartya closed the file and rung the bell.

"Sister Maya, take Shivani to her room. And cancel the rest of my appointments for today."

She opened the case file again. There were very few details given in the file. It just mentioned name, age and address. What had happened in Shivani's life?

She had seen something in Shivani's lifeless eyes. An expression she couldn't decipher. Was it hope of seeing someone? What was it? She was not sure.

But she would find out whatever it was that she had seen. She had to find out and she would. She got up and started pacing the room.

Dr. Amartya was feeling restless and she hated the feeling. Why was this case bothering her so much? All these years she had been able to maintain good control over her emotions while practicing her profession. How was this case any different to her?

Shivani had been admitted last week for attempting suicide. It was a clear case of depression. As a psychiatrist, in the last ten years she had treated many patients suffering from mental disturbance and depression.

Depression cases had increased over the years. Social and work pressure had resulted in the increase in the number of patients suffering from severe depression. Patients usually rambled on about the past or spoke about irrelevant things as if in a trance or stuck in a particular period of time. But Shivani was not responding at all. Shivani too was in a trance and she refused to speak or react. The girl had gone into a deep shell of silence. It was a self imposed silence. A silence that reflected immense hurt and sorrow...Who had hurt the girl so much that she had lost interest in life?

Sister Maya had told her that Shivani hadn't eaten anything for three or four days and had fainted at her residence. She had been admitted to the hospital in a very bad condition. Shivani's silence troubled her. The case had first been handled by the General Practitioner, Dr. Rao who had put her on drip immediately. Within the next two days Shivani had looked okay but the doctor was surprised when Shivani did not speak or answer him.

It was then that the hospital had called up Aparna Mistry, the girl who had admitted Shivani. But Aparna hadn't disclosed much information and the case file was almost blank with just a few comments by the General Practitioner. The previous reports attached showed dehydration and weakness. The reports taken yesterday were showing normal. No physical ailments except mild weakness.

She sat down and opened the case file again. She did not find Aparna's telephone number in it. She called the nurse.

"Sister Maya, weren't you helping out Dr. Rao last week when he was handling Shivani's case?"

"Yes, doctor."

"Aparna was the girl who brought in Shivani to the hospital, right? Could you get her contact number?"

"Yes, doctor. I can get it from the reception. She must have left her contact number in the register."

She decided to call up Aparna and see if she could get some more information about Shivani.

Sister Maya returned in less than five minutes with a slip of paper in her hand. "Doctor, this is the number."

Amartya immediately dialled the number but there was no response. Probably, Aparna hadn't reached home yet. It was better to try again later in the evening.

She got up and put the slip of paper in her bag and walked out of the hospital building. It was a short walk to her resident quarters where she lived.

On the way she wondered what it was about Shivani that was bothering her so much. The case was just like any other case. But still, somehow she felt more responsible and drawn towards the girl.

She took a quick wash, had a light dinner and tried Aparna's number again. It was on the seventh ring that Amartya heard, "Hello."

"Hello, is this Aparna Mistry? I am Dr. Amartya from the Carewell Hospital."

"Oh! Doctor, is everything okay? I mean, is Shivani okay? Is there any problem?" asked Aparna, concern visible in her voice.

"Shivani is better. But she is not normal. She hasn't spoken to anyone since she has been admitted. Shivani is under my care now. I am her psychiatrist. I would be glad if you could reveal some personal details about her. It would aid me in starting her treatment."

"Doctor, I did not reveal much to the GP the other day. Somehow I felt Shivani will snap out of her silence and things will be fine in a day or two. So I didn't feel it necessary to give any personal details that day. I can tell you all that I know about her. Actually, we have been working in the same department for the last two years."

"Aparna, I am sorry to interrupt you. But would it be possible for you to spare some time and come and meet me at the hospital tomorrow? Or, do you want me to meet you outside somewhere? It will be better if we meet personally and discuss the matter."

"I will come to the hospital tomorrow, around 8 a.m. Will that be okay doctor?"

"Yes, thanks Aparna. See you tomorrow then."

Amartya disconnected the phone. So Shivani and Aparna were colleagues and probably good friends too. Tomorrow she would get to know some personal details about Shivani and she could start her treatment. There had to be some reason for Shivani's silence.

There were many questions troubling Amartya. Why had a friend admitted Shivani? Didn't the girl have parents? Was she an orphan? Hopefully, Aparna would be able to clear her doubts tomorrow. Amartya knew instinctively that the case was not as simple as it seemed on the surface.

Chapter 2

Next morning Amartya reached the hospital at quarter to eight. She knew Aparna would not arrive before 8 a.m. She had cancelled most of her appointments for the week and had decided to concentrate only on Shivani's case. She just hoped that Aparna would give her some information which would make Shivani's silence easy to comprehend.

She walked into the washroom and splashed water on her face. There were dark circles under her eyes. She stared at her reflection taking in her appearance. She looked a little like her mom who had been so beautiful. She had inherited her mom's typical Indian features. Her long sharp nose, large brown eyes and black silky straight shoulder length hair were exactly like her mom. But her skin colour, 5'10" height and the way she carried herself reminded her of her dad. She winced as she thought of him. This was not the time. She wiped her face with a tissue, combed her hair, took a deep breath and walked out of the washroom. She knew she looked like an American, like her dad. She adjusted her white sari, and sat on her chair. She liked white...

She heard the discreet knock and knew it was Aparna.

"Come in please."

Aparna walked in nervously. The girl was probably 24 or 25 years old, tall and slightly overweight, complexion on the darker side, black kohl lined eyes and waist length hair which she had tied in a ponytail. She was wearing a white and orange salwar kameez. The girl was simple, yet good looking, thought Amartya summing up the girl.

"Hello Aparna, please sit down and be comfortable. How are you?"

"I am fine, doctor." Aparna sat down and adjusted her dress. She kept her handbag on the table.

"Doctor, could I go and see Shivani? I am worried; I don't know why she is not speaking. She is such a talkative girl. She would even speak to herself if nobody was there. I mean, we all at the office used to tease her like that. Why is she not talking, doctor? What is wrong with her?"

Amartya replied, "Shivani has blocked herself from the world. She can see us, hear us but has decided not to respond. It might not be a conscious decision. She has no problem with her speech or any other physical problem. This happens when a person receives shocking news or faces some emotional setback and becomes depressed. It is like a mental block, a safety barrier. Some or one of our sense organs does not function normally because the brain has lost interest in giving commands."

"Aparna, I would like to know more about Shivani. Tell me whatever you know, anything that you remember about her. Like, for how long have you known her? When and where did you meet her? Her habits, whatever you can recall now tell me."

Aparna took a deep breath and then sighed deeply. Amartya felt as though the girl was trying to muster enough strength to speak about Shivani. Probably, they were very good friends and Aparna was finding it difficult to see Shivani in this state. Amartya waited patiently for Aparna to speak.

Aparna took a deep breath again and then began, "I saw her the first time when I joined the CTC, Commercial Trade Centre. She was talking to some client and I was at the adjoining desk. I couldn't help but overhear the conversation that had taken place between them. She had very intelligently convinced the client and I was impressed and taken a liking for her on the first day itself."

She continued, "And then well, we became friends. I spoke to her, took her advice on office matters and she always helped me out, especially while dealing with clients. She had joined CTC around two years ago and had learnt quite a lot during the time. We both used to have lunch together and I used to share all my personal problems with her. She did not speak much about herself though. It is surprising that I didn't realize it earlier. Now when I think of it, I feel like I used her like a confession box and she hardly spoke about her life. But then she stayed alone and I stayed with my family. She stayed near my house and sometimes I used to see her on weekends. But most of my weekends were busy with family functions and outings."

Amartya asked, "Had Shivani ever mentioned her parents to you?"

Aparna leaned back on the chair and was lost in thoughts, silent for a few minutes. She then picked up the glass of water kept on the table and sipped the water slowly. She continued, "Doctor, she actually never mentioned her parents. Once I remember I had asked her about them and she had said that they were no more and had abruptly changed the topic. I deducted that something tragic had happened in her past and so never raised the topic again. But for that one time, Shivani was always so full of life. She was enthusiastic about everything and everyone in the office just loved her. She was a very kind and helpful person by nature."

Aparna paused for a moment and with bitterness in her voice she continued, "And then Arun came into her life. Arun Mahendra was one of our clients. He had dealings with our organisation and his company was on my list of clients."

Aparna continued, "First time when he had come to the office, he had spoken to me and cleared some of his doubts. Shivani had liked Arun so much, I remember that day after Arun had left, she had asked me to move his file onto her desk. She had said that she would be dealing with Arun. I had been amused. She had openly admitted to me that she had taken a liking to Arun and wanted to be friends with him. I was surprised, but then Shivani always had her own special way of doing things and I actually had no problem with that."

"Next time when Arun came, I guided him to Shivani's desk and then the ball was in her court. Shivani has a very impressive personality and Arun too started liking her."

Aparna smiled as she spoke about Shivani's interest in Arun.

She continued, "Very soon he started frequenting the office much more than necessary. After a while they started going for friendly dates together. I knew that this would lead further and one day Shivani told me that Arun had proposed and that she was very happy."

Aparna suddenly became silent and had a sad expression on her face.

"Aparna, what happened after that?"

"Doctor, everything was fine for a while. But after around two months or so after the engagement, Shivani looked depressed and sad. When I asked her about it, she refused to accept that she was sad and said that everything was okay. Though she spoke a lot about generally everything in life, she never spoke much about her personal life."

Aparna continued in a strained voice, "And then she just stopped coming to work. I thought maybe she was down with flu or something. But when I called her, she said that Arun had called off the engagement and she was feeling low. She told me she would be fine in a week's time and she would join office. She had assured me that she was fine and that I needn't visit her. I thought of going and visiting her during the week but the work schedule and some family obligations left me with no time. Finally, when I did visit her she was in a total mess."

Aparna paused, sipped some water from the glass and continued, "I cursed myself for not having gone earlier. The house looked like it had been hit by a tornado. Clothes, food, plates etc. were lying everywhere. Plates with half eaten food, rotten were lying on the kitchen sink and on the dining table. Shivani looked so weak. I asked her what had happened and she suddenly collapsed. Then I immediately called the ambulance and admitted her to the hospital. When I think of that day I still feel nervous. I always felt Shivani was emotionally strong and a brave girl because of the fact that she lived alone. I still don't know what had happened between her and Arun. I tried calling Arun but he disconnected my calls."

"I should have gone earlier to meet her. I am feeling so guilty now," said Aparna staring into the empty glass in her hand. Her eyes were brimming with tears.

With tears flowing down her cheeks she asked, "Doctor, what could have happened? Will Shivani be normal again? Could Arun have harmed her in some way? Physical abuse or something... He doesn't seem to be that sort of a character. But we just can't be sure nowadays. What to do now doctor?"

Amartya looked at Aparna who was fidgeting with the glass and looked very tense.

"See Aparna, Shivani is suffering from acute depression. The case is slightly complicated. In her subconscious mind she has taken the decision to stop living life normally. So, though she hears and sees us, she cannot respond as nothing actually registers within her. It has happened due to deep hurt or shock. She's lost interest in life and doesn't want to live anymore. Some people lose their mental balance and behave violently while some commit suicide. Shivani just stopped living. She gave in. Like a boat without an anchor, she was waiting to sink. Thankfully, you went there at the right time and rescued her. So, don't feel guilty."

Amartya continued, "Shivani will become normal again. But, I can't tell how long it will take. It will take time but I won't be taking any rest till I bring Shivani out of this turmoil. Don't worry Aparna, she is safe here."

Aparna sighed deeply. She kept the glass on the table and leaned back on the chair.

Amartya asked her, "Can you give me Arun's telephone number?"

"Sure doctor," said Aparna writing down the number on the notepad.

"Thanks Aparna, you have been of great help. I will call Arun and try to find out why he called off the engagement. Probably that will give me a clue to Shivani's behaviour."

After Aparna left, Dr Amartya stared at the telephone numbers. Aparna had given her Arun's cell number as well as his office number. Arun Mahendra owned a company and dealt with CTC. So far she had only this much information about him.

She dialled his number. He answered immediately.

"Hello, is this Mr. Arun?"

"Yes, may I know who is calling?"

"I am Dr. Amartya from the Carewell Hospital. I wanted to speak to you about Shivani Ghose, your ex-fiancee. She is admitted here in a case of severe depression."

"Oh! Shivani! Well, I am not interested in talking to her or about her. I am through with her. She is not what you think she is, doc. Believe me she is a two faced person. I had a bad experience with her. Are you sure she is suffering from depression or is she just faking it?" asked Arun almost shouting.

Amartya ignored the sarcastic comment and said, "Mr. Arun, I would like to meet you and speak to you about Shivani. I would be highly obliged if you could help me out in this. She is in a bad state and as her psychiatrist I would like to know some personal details about your relationship with her."

"See doctor, I am really not interested in digging into the past. I don't..."

"Please Mr. Arun, I will not take much of your time. I request you to please come and meet me at the hospital. Do think of it as one last thing before you close the chapter with Shivani."

"Well, okay doc. I will come and see you in the evening today."

Amartya disconnected the phone and heaved a sigh of relief. Arun was very angry. Shivani's name had kindled the anger. There was something more to this, something that she did not know about and would find out in the evening. How far was Arun responsible for Shivani's state?

Chapter 3

When Amartya entered the visiting room in the evening, she saw Arun seated on the chair playing with the mobile in his hand. He seemed tensed and restless.

"Hello, Mr. Arun?"

"Yes, doctor." He rose from the chair, shook hands with her and sat down again.

Amartya knew that he was not comfortable and just wanted to get it over with. He was a tall well built man, sported a French beard, was fair, wore spectacles and seemed to have expensive tastes. 'A rich and handsome young man', Amartya observed.

"I am Dr. Amartya John. Please be comfortable. Did you go and see Shivani?"

"No doctor. I am not interested in her at all. I am done with her. It is only for humanitarian reasons that I have come here to help you in Shivani's treatment. That is, if at all she is truly sick. She is a liar."

Amartya was shocked to hear the bitterness in Arun's tone.

"Arun, I wanted to know how well you knew Shivani and the reason for your break-up with her. I hope you will tell me everything. I need some clue to understand Shivani's case. She refuses to speak and is totally depressed."

Arun said, "Oh, I first saw her at the office. I mean CTC, that is, her office. I had some dealings with them. I run a business and we deal with CTC. She was very efficient and I was impressed with her work and her beauty… I fell for her. I should have known not to judge a book by its cover."

“Anyway, we became friends and then I proposed to her. I truly liked her and she too seemed to like me a lot. I called up my parents who stay in Delhi and informed them about my relationship with Shivani. They came here, saw her and were very happy with my choice. We got engaged.”

He took a deep breath and continued, “But after around two months or so, after the engagement Shivani started behaving in a strange manner. She didn’t laugh or was not as happy as she used to be earlier. She had that sad look on her face most of the times. I wondered what had gone wrong and asked her if someone had hurt her sentiments during the engagement ceremony. She had denied that and said that everything was fine. But soon her behaviour changed drastically. Somehow, I started feeling that the girl I had been engaged to and this Shivani were two different persons altogether.”

Amartya noticed that Arun was getting hyped up and emotional. He was still holding on to the hurt and was feeling lot of resentment about Shivani. Though he said that he was through with the relationship, Amartya knew that he was still attached to Shivani. Or probably it was his ego which had taken a beating.

He continued, “I started pestering her. I kept on asking her why she was behaving like that and what had happened to the sweet and lively Shivani I had known. Finally, one day she broke down and confessed.”

Arun suddenly stopped talking.

“Arun, what did she tell you?”

He stared at the painting on the wall behind her.

Still staring at the painting he replied, “She said that there was a man in her life who had been like her guiding star and that he had disappeared. I was shocked to hear that there was a man who she had been seeing and had never mentioned about so far. She then told me that whenever she was in trouble or upset, the man would come and console her and that he had helped her in taking all the major decisions in her life. She revealed that she had been seeing him for a long time now. I couldn't digest the information at all. I asked her where that man was now and she started crying and wailing and lost control. She said he had just gone away somewhere and she didn't know where he had gone and she missed him. I felt like a fool. I sat there listening to her and then finally lost my head."

He stopped staring at the painting and looking at her, he continued, "Imagine doc, she had been having some relationship with another man and I had been taken for a ride. I felt cheap and used. I called her names and in a state of fury just pulled the engagement ring out of her finger and left her house. Thank heavens! I did not stay back to listen to more about that man of hers, whoever he was. Surely he must have come back after I left. She had said that he came every time she was sad and upset."

Arun cursed under his breath and said, "I don't know why and how I got involved with such a type of girl. All the time I was seeing her and dating her, she was having a relationship with another man. And I believe this man stayed with her too. Or at least spent most of his time with her, especially at nights when she got home from office. What a fool I was that I never actually saw through the whole thing! She was nicely enjoying two relationships and I didn't know… I feel I have been a big fool actually."

Arun fell silent again and Amartya knew that he was trying to control his emotions. That had been quite an outburst. Probably, he had been unable to tell his friends and parents about Shivani's affair and so had given some other reason for calling off the engagement. Now in front of her, the whole incident had just tumbled out with full fury.

She felt sorry for Arun but was sure that there had been some misunderstanding. Shivani couldn't have been seeing two men at the same time.

"Arun, I am thankful to you for letting me know so much in detail about your relationship with Shivani. I will take up the case in a new light now. She was hospitalized after she collapsed due to weakness. She had not eaten for days together. It was a case of suicidal depression. Aparna admitted Shivani here. Now, Shivani is physically fine but refuses to speak. She has decided to remain silent and has gone into a shell. Her eyes depict deep sorrow. I took up the case as a challenge. Normally, we doctors would give some pills or shots to counter anxiety in the person and then try hypnotism or shock treatment if nothing else works.

But I decided to find out exactly what was troubling her and get to know the root cause before starting any type of treatment. She is not feigning sickness, believe me Arun. She is truly in a bad state."

Arun just nodded. He looked at his watch. He said, "I have said it all, doctor. There is nothing other than this that I know. I am getting late for a meeting."

He walked out. Amartya knew that Arun was battling with the hurt and injustice that he was feeling and would find it difficult to sympathize with Shivani. But he had shed a lot of light into the case.

Chapter 4

Amartya reached the hospital at 7 a.m. Arun's reaction and his words were still fresh on her mind. How far could she trust Arun's statement? Just like a coin had two sides, this story too had another side. Yesterday evening she had heard Arun's side of the story. She couldn't make any deductions based on that. She had to find out Shivani's side of the story. Who was this man anyway? That is, if at all he was there. Arun could have made up the story just to escape from guilt of some wrong that he might have done to Shivani. But like Aparna, she too felt that Arun was not such a character. He had been genuinely hurt. He couldn't have harmed Shivani unless he was suffering from multiple personality disorder.

She went to see Shivani. Sister Maya was on duty. Shivani was sitting on the bed staring out of the window. Amartya went and stood beside the bed observing her patient. The hospital was located on a beautiful campus and there was greenery all around. All the rooms had a good view of the trees outside. Shivani did not seem to be staring at anything in particular. She was just looking outside with a blank expression on her face. Something or someone had hurt the girl very badly... She had to find out if this man existed or whether Arun had just made up a character. Aparna had not mentioned about any man. If there was somebody in Shivani's life other than Arun, surely she would have mentioned about him to Aparna. Or wouldn't she have?

She had to find out more. Shivani refused to answer and at this moment she did not want to hypnotise the girl. She had kept it as her last option. She instinctively decided to go to Shivani's house and check for some clue.

She called the reception to find out if a key to Shivani's apartment was available. She was told that Aparna had deposited the keys at the desk. Amartya picked up the keys and walked out of the hospital. She called a cab and reached Shivani's apartment in thirty minutes.

The flat was in a total mess and was smelly too. Half eaten food, dirty plates and glasses with cockroaches and ants... It was stuffy inside. She went across the room and opened the windows. She covered her nose with her white silk stole and looked around hoping to find some clue about the man that Arun had spoken about. If the man had been a constant visitor, he would have left some clue behind. Maybe a towel, socks, a shirt, something... But if not, then she would have reached a dead end. She would never know if such a man existed until Shivani broke her silence.

Amartya did not find a single clue in the drawing room. There was a television, a sofa set, a rocking chair in the corner, a small dining table near the window, beautiful curtains, and a flower vase – the flowers had dried completely. Shivani had good taste. The decor of the room was simple yet elegant.

She walked towards the bedroom which was on the other end of the long passage. On the right hand side of the passage, she saw the kitchen which looked neater than the drawing room. She saw something on the counter that caught her attention. She entered the kitchen. It was a diary. She opened it. It was Shivani's personal diary...

Amartya flipped through the pages. Though Shivani had not written on a daily basis, she saw that there were many entries. This diary would probably give her a clue about Shivani's emotional state. *If Shivani had the habit of writing diaries, surely there had to be some more diaries, at least of the last couple of years. Shivani might have kept the diaries somewhere.*

Amartya entered the bedroom which was very neat and tidy. The bedcover and quilt all looked untouched. So Shivani had spent more than a week in depression in her drawing room. The bedroom was decorated in shades of light pink and blue. Amartya opened the wooden wardrobe hoping to get some clue. But she found nothing. Clothes were neatly stacked in shelves and some of the dresses were on hangers. There was a mild aroma of lavender perfume inside. Amartya shut the wardrobe door disappointed at having found no clue. She then saw a book shelf which was in a corner of the bedroom. She had almost missed it. The bathroom door covered the area and the bookshelf could have easily gone unnoticed. She tried opening the door but found it locked.

Amartya guessed that there had to be something inside which was of great importance to Shivani. She cupped her hands and peeped in through the stained glass door and saw many books lined in a row. Perhaps the personal diaries were there along with the books. Or maybe some photographs, memoirs...

She started looking for the key everywhere in the room. She searched the drawers, inside the wardrobe, under the pillow but she didn't find the key.

She walked over to the bookshelf again and there she saw on top of the shelf a beautiful white marble statue of a small girl with flowers in her hand. It was beautiful and Amartya couldn't resist touching it. As she slid the statue something fell down. Amartya bent down and picked it up. It was a key. She fitted the key to the bookshelf door and heaved a sigh of relief when the door opened.

Inside there were many novels, self-help and motivational books, some magazines, travelogues etc. Amartya checked the lower shelf and found more than a dozen diaries stacked neatly. If Shivani was 25 years old now, then she was writing a diary since she was 12 or 13 years old. Amartya picked up all the diaries. The diaries would reveal some more information about Shivani. She shut the windows and locked the house, holding the diaries in her arm. She would have to send someone to get the house cleaned, she thought.

She stepped out of the building and hailed a cab. Though she was tempted to start reading the diaries in the cab itself, she resisted. Shivani's case was special and she couldn't afford to make any wrong deductions. She had to go slow and take her time before coming to a conclusion.

She reached the hospital in less than fifteen minutes. There had been absolutely no traffic on the road. She paid the cab driver and walked towards the hospital quarters holding the diaries in her arms. She observed that the building quarters looked old and dowdy from outside. But the rooms were large, airy and spacious. Amartya entered her room and kept the diaries on her desk. She had to freshen up. She decided to take a shower.

She wiped her damp hair with the towel. Her stomach growled with hunger. With the towel tied around her head like a turban, she opened the refrigerator wondering what to make for dinner. She sliced some cucumbers, tomatoes and onions. She arranged the vegetables on slices of bread and sprinkled some salt and pepper. She added some sliced black olives and made a jumbo sandwich. She warmed a glass of milk and added some cocoa to it. She wanted to start reading the diaries and yet she was going about slowly with her chores. She ate the sandwich slowly sipping the cocoa at intervals. Finally she finished the meal, cleared the dishes and picked up the diaries and went inside the bedroom. She counted the diaries. There were fourteen. The older ones had some loose pages and the ink had faded.

She arranged the diaries year wise from 1997 to 2010 and picked up the oldest one. She would read through Shivani's life – the way Shivani would have lived it. She could just pick up the latest one and see if there was some man in her life or what Arun had said or done in the week before she was admitted to the hospital. But Amartya knew that it would not help her understand Shivani's personality. She just hoped that Shivani would have written something about her parents.

Chapter 5

DIARY – 1997

The year 1997 was boldly printed on the diary. Shivani must have been twelve years old. Amartya turned the pages. She knew she was invading Shivani's privacy but she would have to do that to help the girl come out of the mental trauma. The entries were small and not regular and were mainly about her friends at the hostel. She went through the entire diary and towards the end she read one particular entry which intrigued her.

28th October, 1997

Dear Diary,

Today I am feeling very depressed. Today after class Ramya asked me something which hurt me a lot. I know she is my friend and all that but still... She asked me about my mom and dad. Actually her mom and dad had come to see her and she was too excited. So excited that she did not mind hurting me. But after her parents went, she understood that she had unknowingly hurt me. She went on pestering me to be friends again with her. I don't know what happened but I started crying. I then told her that dad had died in an accident when I was seven years old. She also started crying and asked me about my mom. I did not tell her anything after that. I am not in a good mood at all. I don't even feel like writing the diary. I think I will sleep off and tomorrow will be a better day.

So Shivani's father had died in an accident. Though the diary did not have anything else of importance, it had revealed one important thing.

Amartya picked up the next diary.

DIARY – 1998

This one also had irregular entries and just a few lines at times. Amartya read through the entire diary hoping to read something about Shivani's mother. Halfway through she saw an entry which was blotched with water or perhaps it had been tears. The page was crumpled and faded. But she could read the words.

19th May, 1998

I got my periods today. I hate it. I knew about it as they had already explained in class about all this menstruation stuff. But I never expected it would be like this. The school nurse was very kind and understanding. But I still hate this menses. I hope it goes away. The teacher told me that I am a big girl now and that every month I will get this menses for five days. So out of 30 days in a month, five days are going to be yucky. I truly hope and pray I will not get these periods again. Oh God, let it not come for another year at least. I don't want it at all. I mean why should a girl go through all this? Boys don't have to undergo all this... I am feeling very uncomfortable and now I have a headache also. I am feeling so lonely. I have no one to talk to. I will take the medicine the nurse has given and sleep off.

Amartya came to know after reading some more pages that Shivani actually did not get her periods in the next few months. She got her next period after six months in November.

19th November, 1998

Oh dear Diary,

The periods are back again. Well, at least I got a long break! Ramya and Deepanshi are suffering every month. In fact, they got it even before I got it. I got it first in May and they already had it in March. And they have been getting it every month since then. Ha hah... I feel good about that. Hmmm... Today a new girl came to the hostel. Her name is Akanksha. She is a nice girl. She seems to be nice. As the days pass I will know exactly how she is. If she is good I will take her in my group. Let's see...

Amartya did not find any other information which could help her. She was feeling tired and sleepy. She decided to read one more diary.

DIARY – 1999

16th February, 1999

Dear Diary,

I had a fight with Akanksha today. I don't know why I took her in my group. She seemed to be a nice and quiet girl but she has become very talkative now. She goes on chattering all day. I feel irritated with her. And then she said something about me being an orphan. She also passed some comments. How dare she? What does she think of herself? But I felt bad. Even now I am feeling very sad. Why me? How could I tell her that my mom left my dad and me when I was just five years old?

Amartya was shocked to read the entry. Shivani had scribbled over some of the lines after that and then continued writing.

Mom went away with some other man. I overheard some relatives saying so when they had come here to admit me to this hostel. I think she was dad's sister. She was telling someone – 'Shivani's mom ran away with a younger guy.' I don't remember anything else that I had heard. But that sentence stayed in my mind. I don't even remember how mom looked. In fact, I don't remember dad's face also. I just vaguely remember a court case where I was asked to go with dad. And after two years, dad left me too. But he went to heaven, forever and will never come back. I don't even have his photograph. Mom is alive somewhere but she doesn't want me. I also don't want her anyway. I know I am alone and will stay alone all my life…

The entry was stained as though Shivani had cried while writing it. Amartya had finally found some information about Shivani's mother. She closed the diary and decided to continue reading the next day.

She couldn't sleep well that night. The diary entries troubled her. Shivani had been lonely all her life. Arun had mentioned another man. Did that man exist? This thought troubled her. If the man did exist, Shivani must have definitely written about him in at least one of the diaries. Fighting the urge to get up and continue reading the diaries, Amartya tried to sleep.

Chapter 6

In the morning, Amartya decided not to go to the hospital. She had to finish reading the diaries and get on with Shivani's treatment. She called the hospital and requested for a day's leave.

She picked up the diary for the year 1999. Again there weren't too many entries. Shivani had written just a few lines here and there mentioning about her studies, the hostel kitchen, about some teachers and some classmates. She did not get any more information from that diary. She then picked up the next one.

DIARY – 2000

Shivani was in her tenth grade at that time. Amartya read through the diary.

25th July, 2000

I can't believe I am in my tenth grade. All the girls have already decided what stream to choose. I am not sure whether to opt for Science or Commerce. But I hate Mathematics. Specially geometry... I am feeling so confused. I wish I could talk to someone and clear my doubts. I wonder if I should talk to my class teacher about this??? How I wish dad or mom, no not mom, dad was here to help me out in this. But I am an orphan. I don't have parents to talk to. I have so many friends, or should I call them classmates…as I am not quite close to anyone. Everyone is always speaking about vacations, their parents, siblings and relatives. It is all show off! I feel left out. I have no one about whom I can speak. No relatives also. I am feeling miserable…

Amartya read the entries in August, September and finally, she saw an entry in the month of October which was extraordinarily long. Shivani had written almost two pages.

19th October, 2000

Today was the best day of my life. Actually the day started off very badly. The matron scolded me for being late for breakfast in the morning and I had felt very upset. In the class today a career counsellor had come and given a big lecture. The lady had explained about 'making a right choice – choosing the right stream' and it did make things more clear. I was wondering whether to take Science or Commerce. The options were good if I selected the Science stream. With these thoughts in my mind, I reached my room and was thinking about the options, when he came. I don't know who he is. But he is a gem of a person.

He spoke to me for two whole hours. He has such a nice gentle voice. He asked me what I was so worried about. I told him about my doubts and he guided me so well. He was better than the lady counsellor at school.

Good that my roommate has gone home to see her parents or she would have informed the school about him coming to my room and speaking to me. Lucky me! He asked me, 'Where do you see yourself five years later, Shivani? What work would you love to do? Find out your strengths and your interests and you will know which field to choose. And from now onwards you need not worry at all about anything. Any time you have a doubt, you just need to call me and I will speak to you. I am there for you my dear, don't worry at all.'

Oh! I am like you know ecstatic. That's the word. I am feeling like I am on top of the world. Now I have someone who I can speak to whenever I want. He told me he will be coming next week and by then I have to decide on my options.

Actually, in so many years I have never bothered to think about my interests or strengths like he said. Now when I think of it, I really wonder what I see myself doing after maybe five or six years. I know one thing about myself very well. I like to speak and that I can do very well. But I don't want to become a radio jockey or something on those lines. I also like to interact with people. I like it when there are many people around me. But I don't like to talk about personal things. As long as the discussion is based on anything other than personal topics,

I don't mind. I don't like blood, dissection, chemicals etc. So I think opting for Science is out of question. Well, then maybe I should choose the Commerce stream. I will discuss in detail with him when he comes next week. For now I am very happy that I am no longer alone...

Amartya closed the diary. She looked out of the window. The mango tree was laden with green unripe mangoes. She got up and stared at the fruits. Soon they would turn ripe and sweet. She loved mangoes. She had grown up eating more of apples and pears. She sat down on her favourite rocking chair near the window. So there had been a man. Who was this man? How had he entered the hostel?

Maybe he was one of the staff or some new employee... Shivani had trusted the man. She had not mentioned his name, age or looks at all in the diary entry. Amartya felt troubled. She opened the diary again.

The man had visited Shivani again after another week. Shivani had written in detail about the discussion she had with that man. But nothing had been written about the physical appearance and this troubled Amartya a lot.

She went through the diary again hoping to find some description of the man who had visited Shivani. But she was disappointed. She picked up the next diary.

Chapter 7

DIARY – 2001

As she read through the entries, Amartya observed that suddenly Shivani's writing had become bolder and the girl seemed more confident.

20th January, 2001

Next month we have our prelims. I am prepared for the exams and am very confident that I will score well. I am sure about that. He will be coming tomorrow to see me. After discussing in detail with him, I am very confident now that I will be opting for the Commerce stream. I will complete my graduation and also try to study Business Management at the same time. I am sure that I will get a good job and I will earn well. I want to become financially independent. I am tired of the small sum of money I receive from dad's trust. But at least it pays for my education. I want to earn a very good income and want to live a luxurious life. I don't mind working hard for it. I will study and put in my best effort for the finals and try to stand first in my batch... He will feel so proud of me.

This man's presence had given Shivani a lot of confidence. She had not written anything negative about the man so far. But name, age, appearance... Amartya wondered who the man was. What could be his age? Why would he help Shivani and meet her on the sly?

She read another entry written three days later.

23rd January, 2001

Ramya has suddenly started avoiding me. Earlier she used to like me. But now it looks like she doesn't like me anymore. After I started scoring top marks in all the subjects, she is literally avoiding me. I think she is jealous of me. Anyway, I don't care. I am going to just concentrate on my studies and top the batch for sure. I will get the scholarship and that will help me study management. I am very happy he came into my life. He is like the guiding star for me. I will never leave him... And I hope he also doesn't leave me ever...

Guiding star, she had written. It was clear now that this man was the same one about whom she had told Arun. So Arun hadn't been lying. Amartya wondered where this guiding star had disappeared now when Shivani needed him the most.

The entries in the next few months were short and crisp. Probably, Shivani had been busy studying for her board exams. And then one of the entries in June caught her eye.

10th June, 2001

Tomorrow the results are going to be declared. I am feeling very tensed. I hope he comes to meet me tomorrow in the morning. I will feel confident if I see him and speak to him. Deep inside my heart I feel that I will top the merit list and yet I am scared. Oh God! I really really hope he comes...

11th June, 2001

Yes! Yes! Yes! I knew it would happen exactly like this. I am getting the award for best student for this academic year. I have topped the school and my name will be in the local newspaper tomorrow morning!!! I just can't believe it. My hard work paid off. And of course I must thank my darling angel, guiding star. He had come to wish me best of luck in the morning. At that moment I had known that my wish would be fulfilled. Around 4 p.m. the headmistress called me to her cabin. She hugged me and congratulated me and said she was proud of me. I actually can't believe that I have become the centre of attention in school. Everyone wants to speak to me or is speaking about me. Ramya very grudgingly congratulated me. But I don't care. Every student is my friend now. They all want to talk to me. I feel so sure, so confident about myself now. I became like this because of him. Maybe I was always clever and intelligent but I never concentrated on my studies and so never got top rank in class. But after he came and gave me so much confidence, I started feeling that there is nothing difficult in this world. I can achieve anything I want, provided I focus on my goal. And with him beside me, what worry would I ever have now. I am going to be very busy in the next few weeks with the award ceremony and all. Oh! I am so happy... This is the second most beautiful day of my life so far... The first was when he first came in my life!

So Shivani had scored well. Amartya felt like picking up the last diary, 2010 to know more about the man. But she held herself. The suspense was troubling her. But she wanted to follow Shivani's life the way she had lived it. That would give her a clear perspective. It was better to read the diaries in the correct order.

She flipped through the pages and read that Shivani had taken admission in the Commerce stream and had taken Management as her core subject. Shivani had written that the man visited her at least once a week.

Amartya opened the next diary.

DIARY – 2002

Amartya read the diary thoroughly hoping to find some entry where Shivani would have described the man. Surprisingly none of the entries had any description about the man. But the man was a regular visitor. Shivani had been in her 12th grade preparing diligently for the Board exams. She had written a lot about her favourite subjects and her progress in class.

21st September, 2002

Today it was a great day at school. We had a surprise test in Accountancy and I scored the highest. Akanksha has become close to me again. Sometimes I get confused about friends. I never understand who my best friend is. Deepanshi, Akanksha and now many other girls, all are talking so nicely to me and everyone wants to be my best friend. But I still like Ramya and she is the only one who keeps a distance from me. I am happy going to school and attending all the classes.

I just love studying Management and I will join for my diploma in Business Management as soon as I finish my 12th boards. So in the next three years I will complete my graduation as well as my DBM

I wonder how I could have taken all these decisions if he had not been here to guide me. He is like the magic genie. Each time I need to take a decision or I am upset about something, I just have to think of him. Somehow he gets the message as though some magical vibes pass on to him and he eventually comes to meet me in a day or two and helps me out with my problem. I just wish that he will be there for me all my life guiding me all the time...

There were very few entries after that. Amartya opened the next diary.

Chapter 8

DIARY – 2003

Shivani had written that her exams had gone well and that she would have no problem in getting admission in a good college. In one entry she had written that if she scored well, the school would arrange for scholarship which would take care of the fees. In another entry she had written that the headmistress had promised to help her in getting admission in a well-known college with hostel facilities.

Amartya read on and then she came across an entry which troubled her.

27th April, 2003

I never knew that I was so beautiful. But today he had come early in the morning and he told me that I am a beautiful girl. He then told me that I need to realize how beautiful I am. And then surprises of all! He told me to make some changes in my appearance. He told me to go out to the beauty parlour and get a haircut. I have decided to go on the monthly outings day to the beauty salon. I usually go along with my classmates for a movie and shopping. But I don't like it that much. So this time I will spend my savings at the parlour.

I am eagerly waiting for next week when I will get a chance to go out of the hostel. I wish he could accompany me. But I am sure he won't. There will be other girls too with me and he won't come in front of them. He told me not to tell anyone about him or he would just go away. So well, this is my secret and I am never ever going to tell anyone about him.

Anyway, Akanksha will be there with me. I have seen her visit the parlour when we opt to go for a movie. All that is besides the point... I am really really glad that he thinks I am beautiful. None of my friends have ever said that I look good. I always tell the other girls if they are looking cute or good. But I never receive any compliments. Now that will change soon…

Amartya turned the pages slowly reading every entry in detail. She was feeling tired and drained out. She needed a break. She closed the diary. Shivani's diary was revealing a lot about the man's nature but nothing about his physical appearance or age. She decided to go to the park. She changed into light blue denims and a white shirt.

It was just a ten minute walk to the park. There weren't many people around and she walked along the track absorbing the beauty of nature around her. The trees were swaying in the breeze and she crossed her arms to hug herself. It was quite chilly today. She should have taken a shawl. Maybe it would rain. She looked up to see the dark clouds but knew that the breeze would carry the clouds away and rain was improbable. After a while she sat down on the bench and closed her eyes. She could feel the cool breeze tickling her, making her shiver. Nature had its own way of soothing tired nerves. It would be a good idea to bring Shivani out in the open. Amartya got up and started walking towards the quarters.

She made a cup of strong coffee and picked up the diary and started reading where she had left off earlier. The mystery man bothered her. This man was the reason for Shivani's state today and simply she had blamed poor Arun.

Shivani was an insecure girl and not a girl of bad character. She had not believed the allegations that Arun had hurled at Shivani. But the man was real…

Amartya read every word written in the diary. She did not want to miss out any important clue. As decided Shivani had gone to the beauty salon and opted for an entire beauty treatment package. She had been very excited and the man had come and praised her a lot. He had also said that she was the most beautiful girl in the entire world.

Some of the entries revealed that Shivani had become very confident and that many of the girls in the hostel liked her new look.

But her diary writings revealed that there was a feeling of insecurity and fear that existed in the deep recesses of her mind though it was not visible to others.

Some of the entries revealed Shivani's kind and helpful nature. She had written about how she had helped some of her classmates in their studies and in solving their personal problems.

So Shivani had become a popular figure in the school now. Amartya observed that the girl had transformed completely after the man had entered her life. Shivani had scored well and had taken admission in a good college and completed her graduation. The diaries for the next three years had very few entries. Amartya guessed that Shivani had depended less on the diary and more on the man who had become a regular visitor.

The few entries that she had written were mainly about the man visiting her. Shivani must have been busy as she had taken up the diploma course along with her graduation.

Three years had flown by for her. Shivani had completed her Diploma in Business Management (DBM) successfully along with her graduation. She had enjoyed the three years and had not encountered any problems during the time. She had also worked part time with a small trading firm on weekends and had earned enough money for her expenses.

The entries also brought to light a fact that Shivani did not take any decision without consulting the man. He was very important for her and stood like a pillar for her every time she needed him. Nowhere had she mentioned his name though. It was always my guardian angel…

Amartya finished reading the diaries for 2003, 2004 and 2005. She knew that the next diary would reveal Shivani's job details and about her relationship with Arun. She had to get up early tomorrow. She had fixed appointments for some of her regular patients. She decided to retire for the night. Tomorrow it was going to be hectic.

Chapter 9

She got up in the morning feeling very lethargic. She was in no mood to go to the hospital. But there were some appointments that she couldn't avoid. Her mind was on the diaries. She wanted to finish reading the diaries. The thought of the diaries brought instant energy in her and she jumped out of her bed. She would finish her work at the hospital and try to get back early.

She showered and dressed quickly. She adjusted the pleats of the lavender cotton sari. She made some tea and sipped it slowly. She kept the glass in the sink and went inside her room to get her bag. She looked at herself in the tall mirror on the wardrobe. She smiled as she looked at her image. She had never worn a sari before coming to India. But she felt very comfortable wearing saris and had a vast collection of cotton saris in her wardrobe now. She loved the plain ones which had a thin silk border. She instinctively picked up a couple of Shivani's diaries and put it in her bag. She locked the door and walked towards the hospital building.

She settled on her chair, ready for her first appointment. Today, she was seeing her regular patients who had come for a follow up. She had decided not to take any new patient till she had solved Shivani's case. After her last patient left, she mulled over Shivani's case. Why was she finding it difficult to break Shivani's silence? She decided to go and see Shivani.

But on second thoughts she changed her mind and called the nurse.

"Sister Maya, please bring Shivani."

Amartya sat staring at the wall waiting for the nurse to bring Shivani. She had to help Shivani. The girl had to become normal again. Today she would try talking to her and hope that she would react in some way. She had planned out her speech in such a manner that Shivani would have to react. A cry, scream, anger, some emotion... Any reaction would mean that Shivani had come out of her trance and then the treatment would be easier.

Sister Maya knocked before entering. Shivani looked slightly pale today. But Amartya decided to talk to the girl and evoke some reaction out of her.

"Sister Maya, could you please be ready with the shot? I will be trying to provoke Shivani and if she reacts violently kindly be prepared with the tranquilizer."

Amartya looked at Shivani who sat silently, completely unaware of her surroundings. Her eyes stared at the wall seeing nothing. Or perhaps her eyes wanted to see something or someone?

"Shivani, I read your diaries. I know it was your personal possession but I had to read it to find out who was responsible for your state. I had gone to your house and there I found all your personal diaries and I have read most of them," said Amartya.

Amartya took a long pause hoping to see some change in expression on Shivani's face. But Shivani just sat there as if Amartya had not uttered a single word. How was it possible that the girl did not even flicker an eyelid. She sat there like a statue. She refused to eat or drink. She had been on the drip for the last so many days.

"See Shivani, I know there is this guardian angel in your life. Now you have to tell me who he is. I have been unable to get any clue about this man from your diaries. Who is he? Shivani, Shivani!"

Amartya raised her voice slightly but still Shivani sat silently, totally unaffected. Amartya took out the diaries from her bag and placed it in front of Shivani hoping for a response. But Shivani sat there expressionless, without any movement.

Amartya sighed. She asked Sister Maya to take Shivani to her room. After they left, Amartya looked at the diaries and wondered who the man was. Whoever he was, she would have to find out. Would keeping a watch on Shivani's apartment help? Where was he now? Didn't he know that Shivani was in the hospital? Or had he visited her already? Had he harmed Shivani in some way? Maybe he had come after Arun had left and said something or done something which would have caused Shivani's breakdown.

Amartya mulled over her doubts. She called the nurse and said, "Find out who has visited Shivani after she has been admitted. I want the names of all the people who have visited her at the hospital since the day she was admitted. Make a list and bring it immediately."

This man, whoever he was had hurt Shivani so badly that the girl had gone in deep shock. Amartya knew that she might have to hypnotise Shivani and find out the truth. Amartya did not prefer this method but it looked like she was left with very little choice.

She was getting so involved in Shivani's case that she was finding it difficult to see other patients. She had cancelled so many appointments in the last week. Today, she had been able to cover some of the backlog.

The Dean had called her asking for an explanation. She had for a moment felt like telling the Dean that she wanted to drop Shivani's case. But she hadn't said so. Instead, she had requested him to bear with her stating that Shivani's case was complicated and taking up most of her time. Something had held her back. Amartya didn't understand what this 'something' was that was linking her so much to Shivani. Some deep unknown connection...

Chapter 10

Sister Maya gave her the list. Amartya went through the names and saw that most of the visitors had been office colleagues. Last week except for Aparna no one had come to see Shivani. Initially, when she had been admitted many people had come to see her. But after she had been shifted to the psychiatry ward, no one had come. Probably, they felt that Shivani had gone mad or something. Amartya felt sad that there was nobody who actually bothered about Shivani. The girl was truly an orphan.

And then it struck her. No! Shivani's mother was alive. How could she be an orphan? Though the woman had left Shivani and gone away, she still was the woman who had given birth to Shivani and was rightfully her mother.

Amartya decided to find out the whereabouts of Shivani's mother. First, she called Aparna.

"Hello Aparna, could you do me a favour? I wanted to know if you could get hold of Shivani's personal detail file from the office. I would like to know the name of the hostel where she had stayed while studying. Just check the educational certificates that she would have submitted after getting the job."

After half an hour, Aparna called and gave her the name of the hostel where Shivani had stayed. The hostel records would have some details of Shivani's parents or some relatives. She was determined to get to the root of this.

She then called up the hostel where Shivani had stayed. After a lot of explanations, finally she was connected to the Headmistress who informed her that she had the telephone number of one relative mentioned in the register. The Headmistress had been appointed recently and had no idea who Shivani was. Amartya thanked the woman for the number and disconnected the call.

Amartya stared at the number and name she had scribbled on the notepad. The number belonged to Shivani's paternal aunt, Mrs. Mrinal Sen. Amartya picked up the phone to call Mrinal Sen.

"Hello, yes?"

Amartya could make out from the voice that the woman speaking on the phone was aged.

"Hello, I am Dr. Amartya from the Carewell Hospital and I wanted to speak to Mrs. Mrinal Sen about Shivani."

The woman did not respond immediately and Amartya could hear her breath which was quite loud. Amartya waited for the woman to speak.

"I am Mrinal Sen. What do you want?"

'*Oh God, finally!*' thought Amartya. She spoke, "Mrs. Mrinal, I am a psychiatrist. Shivani is suffering from mental shock and depression and is under my care. I would like to know some details about Shivani's parents. If you could tell me where you stay, I could come and meet you. Shivani refuses to speak and is in deep shock."

Amartya continued, "I am unable to find out the reason for her silence and I don't want to try shock treatment therapy now. Any information from her past could help me in understanding the reason for her shock and could make the treatment process simpler."

Amartya paused for a moment hoping to receive a positive answer.

Mrs. Mrinal replied, "See, I have not been in touch with Shivani for ages now. When all other relatives had deserted responsibility of the girl, I had taken her and put her in a hostel. I had deposited all the money that my brother had left behind along with his life insurance remittances into a trust. I am sure the money would have lasted well for her education purposes and till she turned eighteen after which she could handle the account. This is all I know and I can't help you any further than this. I don't know what she has been doing in the last fifteen or sixteen years."

Amartya felt that the woman was going to disconnect the line.

"Please Mrs. Mrinal, I would not take much of your time. Not more than fifteen minutes for sure. If you give me your address, I could come and meet you."

Amartya wondered why the woman was trying to avoid her. But she knew that she would get some important information from her. She had no idea what the information was going to be but she would meet her and find out.

Amartya jotted down the address which Mrs. Mrinal reluctantly gave. She got up, took her bag and decided to go and meet Mrs. Mrinal immediately before the woman changed her mind.

Mrs. Mrinal stayed on the other end of the town and it took more than an hour for Amartya to reach the address. She rang the bell. After what seemed like around five minutes, the door opened.

Amartya looked at the old woman who had opened the door. The lady was in her late sixties, she guessed.

"I am Dr. Amartya John. I had called you a while ago to speak about Shivani."

The old woman was wearing a beige cotton sari which was slightly crumpled as it had not been starched. She stared through her spectacles and then opened the door widely. Amartya entered the house which was very old and not kept quite well. Maybe Mrs. Mrinal was alone and financially not well off, she assumed.

"Please sit down doctor. I am not keeping good health and have memory lapses at times. I am not sure I can help you much about Shivani, but you can ask me whatever you want. I will answer whatever I remember."

Amartya looked at Mrs. Mrinal and observed that there were many wrinkles on the woman's face and she looked older than her age. The room was semi dark with dark red, thick curtains pulled across the windows. There was a dim light flickering on the ceiling and an old fan which creaked as it turned. The house had an ancient look and Amartya observed that there were many antique statues kept in the wall unit across the room. There was an old model television and she could hear a faint melodious sound coming out of a tape recorder.

Amartya sat down on the single seat sofa and kept her bag on the centre table. She decided to come to the point directly.

"Mrs. Mrinal, I want to know whatever you can recall about Shivani's father and mother."

"My brother… Amar… Oh! He was a gem of a person," Mrs. Mrinal exclaimed.

After a pause she continued, "But his wife was terrible. She never loved him. Amar was mad to have fallen for that woman and married her. We had all told him not to marry Ragini. But he was very young and he didn't listen to us. All relatives stopped talking to him after he married Ragini. I used to call him up often. But my husband did not approve and disliked the fact that I was in touch with Amar. Everyone was angry with Amar and he had become the black sheep of our community."

She continued, "Ragini belonged to a lower caste and did not belong to our community. And true to our beliefs, she left Amar for another man. Amar was devastated and shocked. He lived only for his daughter Shivani. For him his entire life and existence was Shivani. The court had no choice but to give Shivani's custody to Amar as Ragini had run away and had lost all rights on her daughter."

Mrs. Mrinal started coughing. She got up and poured a glass of water from the jug on the table. She then took a tablet from a square white plastic box and gulped it down with the water. And as an afterthought she asked, "Would you like to have some water?"

Amartya said, "No thanks. I am good."

Mrs. Mrinal then said, "Where was I? Yes. Well, Ragini went away. For two years father and daughter lived happily. I told Amar to remarry but he was adamant. He didn't want to bring a new mother for Shivani. But I think he was heartbroken and still loved Ragini. Everything was going well in their life and then suddenly Amar died in a horrific car accident after a couple of years. There was no one to take care of Shivani and my husband would never have allowed me to bring the girl home. He had broken all contact with Amar after the marriage and did not know that sometimes I used to speak on the phone with Amar. I never told my husband. After Amar's death, I took Shivani to the hostel and made arrangements for the girl's education. A couple of my friends helped me in this. My husband never knew about it. He still doesn't know."

Amartya listened to Mrs. Mrinal who had spoken continuously as if she would lose track of her speech if she stopped in between. So Shivani's mother's name was Ragini Ghose.

"Is there any way to know where Ragini is now?" asked Amartya.

In an outraged voice Mrs. Mrinal said, "That woman destroyed my brother's life. I was happy when she left him and had hoped Amar would remarry some girl from our community. But he had refused to discuss about it. He had loved only Ragini and he was very concerned about Shivani. So he had stayed single after the divorce. Amar had been shocked when Ragini had one fine day just said that she was in love with someone else. And when Amar had threatened her to stop her relationship with the other man, she had just left the house and gone away. I wonder how a mother could leave her five-year-old daughter and such a loving husband and just go away. I hate her."

Amartya felt a constriction in her throat. Tears were flowing from Mrs. Mrinal's eyes. She wiped her face with the tail end of her sari and still sniffing she continued, "And the man with whom she ran away was none other than Amar's friend, Mithun Dubey. I knew Mithun very well as he was Amar's friend from his college days. Mithun was younger than Amar and in college he had been his junior. Ragini and Mithun were of the same caste. Amar never doubted his friend or his wife and eventually, Ragini left Amar and went away with Mithun. That woman was having an affair with Amar's friend right under his nose. I knew she was not of good character. She had been brought up by her maternal uncle and aunt. No good family background. No wonder she did what she did. Poor Amar… She trapped him and he fell for her and suffered so much."

Amartya looked at Mrs. Mrinal who sighed rubbing her eyes with her hands.

"What is wrong with Shivani? She must be 25 or 26 years old now, right?" Mrs. Mrinal asked all of a sudden.

And then with urgency in her tone she said, "Doctor, you please ask me whatever you want to know before my husband gets back as he won't like it if he knows you are here to speak about Amar or anyone connected to him. He loses his temper at the slightest of things and he has already had two heart attacks."

Amartya said, "I am very thankful to you for the information you have given me, Mrs. Mrinal. Shivani is suffering from mental shock and does not speak to anyone. I wanted to find out more about her past before I start proper treatment on her. I also wanted to know about Ragini, I mean about Shivani's mother and her whereabouts."

Mrs. Mrinal said, "I have no idea where Ragini or Mithun stay. They left Kolkata after the divorce. But I heard from some of my friends that they had seen Mithun perform in a program on television. He is a TV personality, not very famous though."

Mrs. Mrinal looked at Amartya as though pleading her to leave. Amartya took the hint and after thanking the lady she left the house.

Chapter 11

She waved a cab. "Carewell Hospital, please," she said and sat inside. There was very little traffic, she observed. Good, she would reach the hospital sooner than she had expected. She had lots to do. She would have to find out Mithun Dubey's number and contact Ragini. Would Ragini be interested in knowing about Shivani?

Mrs. Mrinal had spoken negatively about Ragini. Why had Ragini left Amar who had been a gem of a man according to his sister? Only Ragini had the answer to this. Amartya knew that speaking to Ragini would answer most of her questions.

She decided not to go back to the hospital and directly went to the quarters. She was feeling very tired. She would have to cancel the evening appointments today. She was getting too involved in Shivani's case. She felt like a detective doing all the groundwork. But she knew it was necessary as she empathized with Shivani who had no one who loved her enough to take care of her. Yet, why was she getting so obsessed with Shivani's case?

Amartya herself had no answers to these questions and wondered if she should surrender Shivani's case to her senior. Her instincts told her that she was the person who had to treat Shivani. Initially, it had been a challenge for her but now it was getting personal. She was thinking of Shivani all the time. And she was not getting sufficient time to concentrate on her other patients who needed her too. She decided to ask the Dean for a break from her other cases and concentrate on Shivani's case. Now, her mind was set on finding Mithun's contact details. She decided to Google search Mithun Dubey. If he was a TV personality, then surely some information was bound to be there on the internet.

'Mithun Dubey', she typed and clicked 'search' and waited for the results. She knew there will be many Mithun Dubeys and it would not be an easy task to locate the one she wanted. After a couple of wrong tries she found – *'Mithun Dubey, singer who was on a recent TV show in Mumbai…'*

Yes! This had to be him. She got the name of the channel on which the show had been aired. She would call up and find out Mithun's personal or office telephone number tomorrow morning.

Next morning Amartya woke up with a headache. She had been unable to sleep and had spent a restless night. She hadn't read the diaries last night. Her mind was on Ragini. She had to contact her and speak to her about Shivani. But that was not what was troubling her. Something other than Shivani was troubling her. She knew what it was but she did not want to think about that now. Her focus had to be on Shivani and she did not want to waste time or emotion on what was troubling her now.

She waited until 10 a.m. before calling up someone in Mumbai. She first called the reception desk of the TV channel and finally after a lot of enquires, she was able to get Mithun's residence number. Hopefully, she would get to speak to Ragini directly. What would she tell her? Amartya knew that she would have to be very tactful while talking to Ragini. She was not sure how Ragini would respond.

The woman who had so easily left her baby daughter to go away with some other man, would she be now interested in knowing about her daughter after twenty years or so? But Ragini was Shivani's mother. There was no harm in calling up and finding out if Ragini was interested in knowing about Shivani. Amartya decided that only if Ragini was interested in knowing about Shivani, she would tell her about Shivani's condition. Otherwise, she would simply disconnect the phone.

Amartya dialled the number. The phone rang five times before she heard,

"Hello?" a lady said.

Amartya hoped it was Ragini on the other end.

"Hello, I am calling from Kolkata. I am Dr. Amartya and wanted to speak to Mrs. Ragini please."

"I am Ragini. Yes doctor, what is it?"

Amartya could sense tension in Ragini's voice. Probably because she had mentioned that she was calling from Kolkata. Ragini's abrupt 'what is it' depicted urgency in her tone.

"See, Mrs. Ragini, I wanted to talk to you about something very personal and I hope that it is okay to talk now. If you were in Kolkata I would have come and met you and had a direct face to face talk. But you are located in Mumbai and it is not going to be possible. So I will have to talk on the phone. Is that okay with you?"

"See doctor, I don't know who you are and why you are calling. I don't have many people who I care about in Kolkata, yet I would like to know what this personal thing is that you want to talk to me about?" asked Ragini.

Amartya knew Ragini was getting more and more worried by the minute. Her tone was fearful and Amartya wondered what it was that Ragini was afraid of.

She answered, "See, I will come straight to the point. I wanted to talk to you about your daughter Shivani. If you are interested I have something to tell you. If not, let us just end the conversation."

There was a long pause on the other end and Amartya wondered if Ragini had actually forgotten about Shivani. How could a woman forget about the child she had given birth to? Or maybe she had children from her second marriage and she did not want any disturbance in her family now.

Ragini started crying. Amartya waited patiently now. She knew the woman on the other end had become emotional on hearing about her daughter after twenty years. If she had even a little emotion for her daughter, then how had she suppressed all that over the years?

"Doctor, how is Shivani. She must be twenty-five years old. Does she know about me?" asked Ragini.

"Mrs. Ragini, Shivani is not in a very good condition now. She is at the hospital admitted for mental depression. She is under my care now."

Amartya knew that Ragini still had some emotions left for her daughter and so deemed it right to give this much information.

"How come she is in such a situation? Has she married? Is Amar not able to help her?"

Amartya wondered in which world this woman lived. She had absolutely no idea that her ex-husband had died years earlier.

"Mrs. Ragini you seem to have drifted away too much from your past. Amar died when Shivani was seven years old," informed Amartya.

"How is that possible? No one informed me. My Shivani... Oh God," Ragini screamed.

Ragini was literally wailing on the phone and Amartya waited for her to calm down.

"I am coming to Kolkata. Doctor, which hospital are you calling from? Where is Shivani admitted?"

Amartya disconnected the phone and sighed. She had given Ragini her address and telephone number. Ragini had promised that she would be there in two days time. Ragini's reaction had actually come as a surprise for Amartya. How come Ragini had not known of Amar's demise?

She got ready to go to the hospital. She had time to see some patients today. As she draped the lemon yellow chiffon sari with a white and gold border, she hoped that Ragini would prove to be of some help. But she still did not have any idea about the man who used to come and meet Shivani. There were five more diaries that she hadn't read. She held the sari clip between her lips as she made the pleats on her sari.

She needed to know in detail about Shivani's past. She pinned the sari clip neatly and looked at herself in the mirror. She combed her hair and tied it with a rubber band. She didn't look good with her hair tied back. She pulled out the band and tossed it on the dressing table. What had actually happened in Shivani's life?

She took her bag and locked the door, lost in thoughts. She walked towards the hospital building thinking about Shivani's case. In her past experience she had observed that more than medicines and treatment, it was always helpful if the patients' personal issues were researched. Always in psychiatric cases, the root cause lay in the past or some mental trauma caused by someone, generally a close relative. Many a time external factors like financial losses, business ups and downs also left some people mentally unstable but even in such cases, the root cause would hint at some past experience which caused the instability in the present situation.

She reached the hospital. After seeing her patients she would go and meet the Dean. By mid-afternoon she was free and she went to meet the Dean. She came to the point directly and told him that she wanted to concentrate on Shivani's case and so couldn't take up other cases for a while. She did not reveal too many details about her research on Shivani's past. The Dean agreed to give her full charge of Shivani's case. It had taken a lot of convincing though. Amartya walked out and heaved a sigh of relief.

Now her mind was focused on Shivani and she hoped that Ragini's arrival would make a difference. Two days would just go by…

Amartya decided to continue reading the diaries. She still had to find out Shivani's side of the story.

Chapter 12

Amartya reached home after 8 p.m. She showered quickly and went directly to the bedroom. She was not feeling hungry. So she decided to have a late dinner. She picked up the next diary...

DIARY – 2006

Shivani had been in her final year and had got good results. She had become very confident and independent after that man had come in her life. Amartya wondered what kind of relationship the two shared. Somehow she never felt that Shivani was physically involved with that man. But why was that man always around? What was the reason behind his kind gestures? Nobody did anything simply. He had made the girl dependent on him. But at the same time he had helped Shivani in taking all the decisions in her life. He had helped her become confident. This man was an enigma.

5th July, 2006

I got a job! I am so happy today. And the best part is while everyone is struggling away trying to get a good job, I clinched one right away. The trading firm where I was working part time has an account with the Commercial Trading Centre where I got placed. I am really very happy that now I will be totally financially independent! First thing I will do is leave this hostel and rent a flat of my own. The salary they have offered at CTC is much more than I had expected.

But the person who recommended my name had seen my work and had sent in a reference. Well, whatever it is, I am now set to move out on my own. I really hope he will come today. I have to tell him the good news.

He had assured me that I will be able to get a good job very soon and that I could soon move out of here. I hope he comes with me for house hunting as it could be quite a tedious process. I am going to be staying in a house of my own finally. No hostel matrons, no rules and regulations…

Amartya realized how suffocated Shivani must have felt all these years staying in a hostel. The girl had wanted freedom badly. Freedom from the rules at the hostel, freedom to go and come anytime and anywhere she wanted and freedom to meet the man whenever and wherever she pleased…

As Amartya continued reading the diaries, she learnt that Shivani had rented a cosy one bedroom apartment in a good locality. The building where she had rented the flat was not very far from her office. She would take a bus and reach in fifteen minutes. She was happy with the work atmosphere at the office. Her boss was good and liked her a lot. All in all Shivani was independent in every way except for her dependence on the man. She had become emotionally dependent on him. Her entries revealed how at times she missed not having somebody with whom she could live her life with. She wished to meet a nice guy who she would marry and live a secure life. The man still came to meet her, now more often as she was staying independently.

Amartya looked for some hint about the man, his name or something in the diary entries but found none. Why had Shivani kept the identity of this man a secret even in her personal diary which she kept locked in the bookshelf? Amartya was puzzled and not quite able to understand the mystery of the man and Shivani's possessiveness about him.

So the year 2006 had passed nicely for Shivani as she had completed her graduation, acquired a job and rented an apartment. So when had she met Arun? Arun had come to CTC after Aparna had joined. Probably, after 2008… She picked up the next diary.

DIARY – 2007

Shivani hadn't written much in this diary. Just that her job was going very well and she felt happy that she could spend as much as she wanted. She had received a raise and was in for a promotion too. Her boss was pleased with her work and had given her several letters of appreciation. At times her entries were just a few lines where she mentioned about her loneliness. She worked as long as she could at the office – *the thought of coming to an empty house was quite dreadful.* But at times she had written that she was eagerly waiting for the day to get over so that she could reach home as 'he' was coming.

30th November, 2007

He had come today. I felt so good. We talked for hours together. I went on and on about my boss, my office and he just listened with a smile on his face. He is so nice. I am glad that he comes to meet me even now. Earlier I was afraid that he would stop coming once I move into my own flat.

But he comes regularly and I am happy about that. Just that I wish he would stay here with me all the time so that I would not feel the fear, the insecurity which I feel when he goes away and I am alone…

Shivani's life revolved around that man and her office. Though she was now on her own feet literally, she was still holding on to that man for her security.

DIARY – 2008

Amartya stared at the diary. She was not so sure about this man and his involvement with Shivani. She opened the diary and started reading the entries. Shivani had written about Aparna in some of her entries.

27th January, 2008

A new girl has joined the office today. Her name is Aparna Mistry. She seems to be good and my age almost. She is very tall though unlike me. Well, I am not too short. Now 5' 4" is quite okay. Anyway, maybe we will be friends. I truly hope so. All the others at the office are so old and I feel like a kid. She will be sitting in the same cabin where

I sit. Though she is new to CTC, she has some previous experience from some other company. We both will be holding the same profile. Looks like my workload will lessen a bit now. Anyway I am happy.

Amartya went on reading and found out that Shivani and Aparna had become good friends. Shivani had helped Aparna settle in and now they shared the workload of the innumerable clients that CTC handled. They both worked like a team and the boss was very happy with their work. At times Aparna visited Shivani as she stayed nearby.

16th August, 2008

I dread the weekends as I have no idea how to spend the day doing nothing. I tend to laze around and feel lonely by afternoon. I do the laundry, try to cook something with the help of the cookbook, arrange my wardrobe... but that's all I have to do and I feel bored. But today Aparna had come home. We both had a good time. She is a sweet girl. At times I miss my hostel friends, Akanksha, Ramya, Deepanshi and all. But we lost contact after we quit the hostel. I have no idea now where they are. But I am glad that I have a good friend now. Aparna and I went for a movie in the evening and then roamed around at the mall, had ice cream and I reached home just a while ago. It is good that Aparna stays in the next lane. I feel good about it. She can come and visit me anytime. I too can go to her house, but there are so many people in her house. She lives in a joint family with her uncle, father, mother, brother, brother's wife and kid... Oh God! So many people! How would it be to live in such a big family? I actually have no idea. But at times I feel I too should have been born in a big family with many people in the house and it would have been a lot of fun. Aparna doesn't have time on weekends as she is always busy with some family function or party or something or the other. Today she was free and so she came to meet me. He was supposed to come today. Had he come when I was out with Aparna? He comes only on Sundays because he knows I feel lonely and bored. He tells me to go for movies and make more friends. Though I interact with so many people, making friends is not very easy. Friends usually ask personal questions and I feel very uncomfortable. I am glad that I have Aparna now. She is a nice girl. It is not so late and I hope he comes to see me tonight before I sleep off. I just hope...

The handwriting was scrawled as though Shivani had slept off writing the diary. Aparna finished reading the diary for the year 2008. So the man came and met Shivani at the apartment. Shivani had never mentioned about this man to Aparna. Obviously, Aparna did not know about the man.

Amartya wondered why Shivani was keeping the identity of this man a secret. Was it because he had told her *not to tell anyone about him or he would stop coming*? Probably that was the reason. But someone must have seen this man come up to the apartment and meet Shivani. Should she enquire with the neighbours?

Chapter 13

She got up and went inside the kitchen. She felt like drinking spicy masala tea. She kept the saucepan on the gas stove. She crushed a piece of ginger, one cardamom, a pinch of cinnamon powder and added it to the boiling water. She added the tea leaves and a teaspoon of sugar. She stared at the tea boiling on the stove. It was black. She then added some milk. She poured the tea in a mug. She knew she was doing everything mechanically. Her mind was on Shivani and her diary entries. She picked up the mug and sat by the window, sipping the tea thinking about Shivani's emotional weakness. But then Shivani was a girl who had been left in a hostel at a young age by some relatives after the death of her father. A girl whose mother had left her when she was just five years old and had been taken care of by her father who had left her too… Shivani had been totally alone as none of her relatives visited her. Who had then paid her expenses? Amartya recalled reading in one of the entries – *'the money from dad's trust is taking caring of the fees'*.

Shivani's father had left behind a good sum of money and the Life Insurance remittances added together might have easily taken care of Shivani's expenses. She had received some scholarships too. The girl was hardworking and intelligent. Amartya felt bad that none of the girl's relatives had bothered to visit her at the hostel. The mother too had never bothered to find out about her daughter? What kind of mother was she?

Amartya felt very restless as she imagined Shivani's life. Her own life too had been not so good. But this was not the time to think of her past. Shivani needed help and proper treatment. Amartya finished the tea and picked up the next diary and started reading it.

DIARY – 2009

Amartya read through the diary waiting to read the entry where Shivani would have mentioned about meeting Arun.

15th September, 2009

I am immensely happy today. I don't know how to express my happiness. I feel like I will go crazy... I met Arun today – Arun Mahendra. Hmmm... He is so handsome and smart. He had actually come to the office for some work. He is our client, the owner of a company and looks rich! He had work with Aparna but he was casting glances at me. I liked him too. Haven't seen such a handsome man for a long while now... Well, he is fair, tall, sports a French beard and wears spectacles. I felt like... my God... I felt way too much after seeing him only once. I have never felt like this before. Is this love, I wonder? Love at first sight? I am not sure. I really don't know.

He has business dealings with our office and I will surely be seeing more of him. I have told Aparna to send his files on my table and I will deal with him henceforth. Maybe he will like me too!

Amartya smiled. Shivani had fallen for Arun the first time she had seen him. Arun was handsome, no doubt about that and for Shivani it had been love at first sight. Amartya read through and learnt that Arun started frequenting the CTC office. That is exactly what Aparna and Arun had told her.

Shivani had written how she had managed to take up Arun's file onto her table by requesting the boss. She had wanted Arun to deal with her.

Amartya closed the diary and kept it on the table. Shivani had beautiful large doe like eyes. Not very tall, but very fair and had long brown hair which curled at the ends. Shivani looked like a Goddess. She had a sharp nose, full lips and long artistic fingers. She was extremely beautiful. An example of a perfect Indian beauty!

Amar must have fallen head over heels in love with Shivani. Any man would...

Love was truly blind. Who would know it better than her? She had also fallen for someone just the way Shivani had and her life had become a disaster thereafter. Not entirely though. In the beginning love is like a bud waiting to blossom and then it turns into a beautiful flower, innocent and waiting to be plucked. But as soon as it is plucked, it starts depending on external factors like a vase to stand in, a sprinkle of water and a ton of love. The life of the flower depends on how lovingly it is taken care of. In rough and unloving hands, the flower soon dries and becomes lifeless...

Every love story was different. But almost always the reason for love to wither was the feeling of insecurity in one partner. The fact that Shivani felt secure with the other man had hurt Arun's ego.

One thing that surprised her was that Shivani had written a detailed description of Arun in her diary. She had mentioned about Arun's physical appearance, age and everything, but had never mentioned a single detail about the physical appearance of the man who came to meet her. Not even his name...

Amartya took the diary and sat on the rocking chair by the window.

31st December, 2009

It was the most fabulous day of my life – I had gone out with Arun and he is such a gentleman. He took me to the Ritz hotel at the City Centre and we had a great time. We danced too. I hope we meet more often. I like Arun and I think he likes me too. Obviously he does. He did take me out to dinner. He held my hand a couple of times. His hands are so soft and I felt something. I loved the feeling and I think I am in love with him, it feels like the whole world is so beautiful. The way he looks at me sometimes... His eyes... I don't know but I feel like he is attracted to me. He hasn't said anything so far, yet I feel he likes me a lot… A happy new year to me!

The diary revealed that Arun and Shivani met many times especially on weekends. They watched movies, visited malls and always Shivani enjoyed herself. Her entries revealed that she was happy.

So, what had happened to that man who used to come and meet Shivani? Didn't he mind Shivani meeting Arun? She picked up the last diary. And then she came across an entry which answered her doubts.

Chapter 14

DIARY – 2010

25th March, 2010

All my life I have had him to guide me, help me and now since I met Arun, he has stopped coming. I am very upset. I hope he comes. I want to tell him that even when I marry Arun I will still need him. He has to come and guide me like he has done for so many years now. Where has he gone? I am feeling terribly low and lonely. I want him to come and see how happy I am with Arun. He comes only when I am depressed. He has always seen me stressed, worried or crying. Now I am happy and I want him to see me like this for a change. I have been busy all weekends meeting Arun. Maybe he must have come and gone. I won't go out anywhere next Sunday. I want to see him and mainly I want him to see how happy I am…

So Arun's entry in Shivani's life had troubled the man. He had stopped visiting Shivani. Any normal person would have felt jealous. Shivani was emotionally dependent on him. If he stopped coming, would she be able to cope? Shivani needed to let go of this man and move on in life, especially now after meeting Arun.

3rd May, 2010

Arun proposed today! I am on cloud nine. I said 'Yes' and I am feeling special. Arun has spoken to his parents and they are coming from Delhi to meet me this weekend. I am glad that finally I will have someone whom I can call 'mom', 'dad'. So what if they are Arun's parents? He told me I must call them 'ma' and 'dad' just like he does. Arun is such a nice person.

I am really lucky to have met him. I will have a family now… He gave me a rose today and then he surprised me by giving me a beautiful diamond ring. We will exchange rings during the engagement ceremony. I just can't wait for Arun's parents to come. There will be no one from my side. But Arun said it was fine. He doesn't mind and anyway, I have my friends and colleagues.

But my guardian angel has not visited me for a while now. And I wanted him to be there for the engagement ceremony. I haven't seen him for a long time now. He used to come regularly to meet me, every Sunday. But now I am never at home on any Sunday. I can't blame him. I guess he must have come and seen that I am not here and gone away. He will come for my engagement, I am sure. He will come even before that just to see me. He has been a pillar of support for me and he is the reason for my success in life. Without his support I couldn't have reached where I am today and I wouldn't have met Arun also. I owe him a lot and I want to tell him all this when I meet him. Every week I decide that I won't go out on Sunday but I am unable to say no to Arun who makes such elaborate and interesting plans just for me. He used to always come when I was in distress and thankfully, since I met Arun, I haven't cried or felt lonely for a single moment. I love Arun a lot. But I love my guardian angel also. Where has he gone away? He could come and meet me on weekdays or at night also... I miss him so much.

In the next few weeks, Shivani had just penned a few words in her diary. Shopping for the engagement ceremony and meeting Arun's parents had taken all her time. And after the engagement she had written a long entry in her diary.

1st June, 2010

I can't believe it! I am engaged. I keep on looking at my hand and the ring convinces me that I am engaged. Arun's parents are very nice. They have gone back to Delhi and they call me up once in two days. They told me that they were happy with Arun's choice. Things at the office are also going smoothly. Aparna was there for the engagement. In fact, she was the only one. He didn't come. He hasn't come for months now. Maybe he has gone somewhere or is busy with something. Though I am very happy, I feel sad that I haven't seen him for so long. I know he will not leave me and go. But I just wish he comes to see me soon. Maybe this weekend...

Where had the man disappeared? He could meet Shivani at her office or at her home. Why wait for weekends? Had the man left town or was he just avoiding Shivani? Amartya had her doubts about this man. But none of Shivani's entries revealed that she had any doubt about the man having left her. She seemed confident that he would come.

23rd June, 2010

I had an argument with Arun today. Actually in the morning when I reached office, I had some good news waiting for me. The boss decided to give me a promotion which had been due for a long time now. The new designation would mean more responsibility and of course longer work hours. I would have to attend parties and meetings with clients outside the office. I might have to meet clients at their offices or at some five star restaurants. I would be working as the team manager! I was so glad but when I told Arun about this, he was not very happy. He argued with me and then told me not to accept the promotion.

He told me that there was no need for me to go to work and that he earned enough for both of us. I was shocked when he spoke so rudely to me. After reaching home I cried a lot. Why does Arun want me to leave my job? I have worked so hard to reach this position and just because Arun says, why should I leave it? I was very upset and did not attend Arun's call. He called me fifteen times on my mobile. I was hoping Arun would come home and meet me. But he didn't come. Finally, he sent me a SMS saying he is tied up with some clients and will see me tomorrow. Big deal!

But there is one very good thing that happened. He came today. My dear guardian angel... He consoled me and told me not to cry. He said that things will work out right and I must try to convince Arun about the promotion rather than fighting or arguing with him. He told me to tell Arun how important the job was for me and he said that Arun would understand. I am so glad that he came back into my life. I am feeling quite confident now to face Arun tomorrow and solve the issue. He is so sensible and sane. We spoke for a long time. He told me that he had come here and seen that I was happy with Arun, so he hadn't bothered to disturb me. He said he was glad that I had met Arun and was going to marry him. He also feels that Arun is a nice guy. I am feeling better now. If he hadn't come I would have cried all night... But he came and he is very happy for me. Before going he said that Arun will keep me happy and I will have a nice secure future from now on. But I didn't tell him that he makes me feel secure and not Arun. I was planning to tell him so many things. But when I saw him, I just didn't remember any of it. All the time I was talking about Arun, the engagement, my future in-laws... I don't know what I would do without him. I just hope he is there for me all my life...

So the man had come back. Amartya was surprised as to how he knew when Shivani was upset. Did he spy on her or did he stay somewhere nearby? Perhaps in the same building? Amartya was worried and wondered if that man had physically hurt Shivani. He must have done something or said something for Shivani to have broken down so badly. Amartya quickly suppressed her urge to read the last few pages of the diary. This was the last diary she was reading and she wanted to read each and every entry properly and not miss out anything.

25th July, 2010

It is raining heavily. It rained throughout the day. I just love the rain. I feel like everything will work out right when it rains. It is like the sun just melts and the rain pours. The heat of anger thaws when it meets the cool rain drops. I met Arun and he told me that the date for marriage has been fixed for 1st September. It is an auspicious day as per the stars. That is what his parents told him. Anyway, I don't care. I am just happy today. There is so much shopping I need to do. I am very excited. I will make a list of 'things to do' as I have actually only one month in hand. I am so happy. Arun loves me and I too love him a lot. And the best part is today I received the promotion letter. I talked to Arun and he told me to accept it. He is not angry like he was when he first heard of my promotion.

It is the rain. It has melted his anger! Maybe its love... But there is one thing. Though Arun loves me, accepts me the way I am, I still feel insecure. I don't know what it is. Somewhere deep inside I have this feeling of insecurity. I just can't understand it. I can't speak to anybody about it. It is too personal. I just wish my guardian angel would come now. He is so sane and practical. He always has a way out of every problem.

I haven't told him about this insecurity that I feel. He feels that as Arun is there in my life, I will be secure and happy. I just hope he comes and meets me. This time I will tell him clearly that even if I marry Arun, I will still need him. Only he can make me feel secure. Arun can give me love but can't make me feel secure...

So this man had not come again after 23rd June. Almost a month... Amartya was unable to understand the relationship between the man and Shivani. If she felt so secure and loved that man, why did she get involved with Arun? How old was that man? Was he young? Maybe he was an older man. Whoever he was, he was very smart. He came when Shivani was upset and low. He had reduced his visits after Arun had come in Shivani's life. After the engagement, the man had just come once. She continued reading.

5th August, 2010

I don't know why but I am feeling very low. I am terribly upset that he has not come to see me at all. Nowadays, on weekends also I am unable to meet Arun. He is busy with the marriage arrangements. Most weekends he is flying to Delhi to meet his parents. They will be coming only in the last week of August. I made my shopping list and found that I had hardly anything much to shop. I purchased all the saris and clothes I wanted. Thankfully, Aparna came along a couple of times with me for shopping. Now just some more shopping needs to be done. I feel so lonely on weekends. Why is he not coming? It is more than a month since he came last. I really don't know what to do. I am feeling so depressed. Arun had called me in the morning from Delhi. He asked me why I was upset. I did not tell him anything. What could I tell him anyway? He would never understand...

Chapter 15

Amartya couldn't understand why Shivani was not disclosing the existence of the man to Arun. Why was it such a big secret? At least she had not written in the diary that she had told about this man to Arun. Obviously, he hadn't known. That is what Arun had said the other day. The entries further on were very depressing.

15th August, 2010

I am tired and I am not sure what to do. Arun has been pestering me for the whole of last week. He wants to know the reason why I am so depressed. He said that I am not the Shivani he got engaged to. He said so many things. He said that I used to be such a lively person. What Arun said is true. But I can't get back to being myself. I want to see my guardian angel. He has just disappeared, gone away. He hasn't come at all. Last time when he didn't come for a long time, I had been very busy with Arun and had not missed him much. But this time I am feeling terrible. Where has he gone away? I need him so much. I want to talk to him and tell him that only he can give me the security that I want. Arun cannot make me feel secure. I want him to come so that I can tell him all this. He feels Arun is with me and that I don't need him anymore. But he doesn't know how much I need him...

Amartya saw tear stains on the entry. Shivani had cried. She must have been terribly depressed. The next few entries just read – "*God, I hope he comes...I need to see him.*"

25th August, 2010

Everything is over. I am finished. He hasn't come. It was the worst day of my life. Today, finally I told Arun about my guardian angel. Arun had been asking me for a while now and I felt that maybe I should tell him now. I told him how this man has been helping me for last so many years. Arun was very angry and lost his temper.

He asked me so many questions about this man. I just told him that this man makes me feel secure and has guided me, helped me in taking the right decisions. I told Arun that the man was my guardian angel and had suddenly stopped visiting me and that I missed him. Arun lost his temper. I wanted to tell Arun everything in detail about my guardian angel. But he was not ready to listen to me. He called me a slut. He plucked the ring from my finger and walked out. He said, "It's over." And I too feel it's over. Two men in my life whom I depended on are now not there in my life.

I have no one in my life who loves me and no one who makes me feel secure. I am alone. Both have left me. Nobody loves me or cares for me. I am alone. I was a fool. I should have known that people are temporary. Either they leave you or they die. No one is permanent. I was under the belief that Arun and I would live a happy married life. We would have kids. A daughter of my own who I would love all my life. All dreams... My guardian angel has decided that he does not want to see me. So he has left me and gone away. Arun is angry and has broken the engagement. No marriage for me now. No kids. I know I am alone. I am aloneee...

Amartya found it very difficult to read the entry as it was blotched with tears and Shivani's handwriting was also very bad. But it was clear that Arun had left Shivani after she had told him about the other man in her life. The other man hadn't come to see Shivani. At least till 25th August. This entry was the last entry in the diary.

Amartya looked at the calendar on her desk. It was 15th September, 2010. Shivani must have waited for the man to come. She must have felt that because she had been depressed and sad, he would surely come. So had he come? Had he come and said something to Shivani or hurt her physically or... If he had come, he would have come after 25th August and Shivani had not written anything in her diary after 25th. If he had come, why would she be in such a state? She would have found her security. Or had he come and been as rude or offensive as Arun? She had so many unanswered questions.

After a lot of thought, Amartya deducted that the man hadn't come and Arun had left Shivani for good. This had come as a shock to Shivani who had been unable to bear the loss of two men whom she had leaned on for love and security.

Amartya knew that Shivani had hoped that Arun or at least her guardian angel would come back. But both the men hadn't come. After a few days of crying and waiting, she might have stopped eating and unconsciously created a mental block due to the trauma she was facing. She must have opened the door for Aparna hoping it was either Arun or her guardian angel. And when she had seen Aparna at the door, she might have been disappointed and succumbed to her weakness and collapsed. She had been admitted on 3rd Sept, 2010. 1st September the girl was to marry Arun. Two days… Amartya kept the diary on the table.

Her eyes were brimming with tears. She was surprised. She had never in the last ten years of her career cried or felt so much emotion for any of her patients. What was wrong with her?

Deep inside she could feel pain, a sharp wrenching pain which Shivani might have experienced when Arun had left her. Amartya knew what that pain was. She herself had gone through such pain. It had hurt her so much. But it had hurt her mom more. The tears were now flowing freely from her eyes. She stared out of the window not seeing anything at all. Her heart was beating loudly and she could feel the wetness on her cheeks. She let the tears fall…

Chapter 16

When Ragini called her from the airport informing her that she had reached Kolkata, Amartya asked Ragini to come to her quarters. There was no point in calling Ragini to the hospital directly. It was better that she met Ragini and spoke to her before taking her to meet Shivani. Twenty years was a long time...

When Amartya opened the door she saw an elegant woman standing nervously with a suitcase beside her. She was fair, was wearing a dark pink sari, had tied her long hair in a plait and did not look her age at all. She had to be somewhere in her late forties but looked much younger than that. Ragini was a beautiful woman, which explained Shivani's beauty.

"Come in, Mrs. Ragini."

"Hello, Dr. Amartya" said Ragini and came in.

Amartya asked Ragini to keep the suitcase near the desk.

"You can freshen up and then we will talk. The washroom is on the left and you can change inside the bedroom." She wanted Ragini to be comfortable.

But Ragini's expression revealed that she was just eager to find out about her daughter. The eagerness in Ragini's eyes was something Amartya couldn't understand. If the woman had been so curious about her daughter, why had she not bothered to contact her till now?

Ragini sat on the sofa and said, "Doctor, I am perfectly okay and comfortable. Could you please tell me what has happened to Shivani? How is she? Can I see her?"

Amartya explained to Ragini all about Shivani's case not going too much in detail about the diary entries. She just gave a brief outline story to Ragini. She told her that she had spoken to Mrs. Mrinal Sen. Amartya wanted to know what had happened in Ragini's life and why she had left Amar Ghose and Shivani twenty years ago. Her revelation could probably shed some light on Shivani's mental state.

"Doctor, what do you want to know? I will tell you everything that might help Shivani to become normal again."

"See Mrs. Ragini, I would want to know some personal details like what kind of a person Amar Ghose was. Why did you leave him?" asked Amartya.

Ragini leaned back on the sofa and took a deep breath. She began, "Amar was a very nice person. We first met at a social function through a common friend. We fell in love. It was love at first sight. He was very obsessed with me and fought with his family and married me. His family members were against our marriage. I had lost my parents when I was very young and had grown up with my maternal uncle and aunt. They were also not happy with my choice and immediately disowned me. I didn't mind. But Amar felt bad when his relatives disowned him. Even his own sister, Mrinal *di* didn't support him."

"After a year when Shivani was born, his joy knew no bounds. He was absolutely crazy about Shivani and somewhere I started feeling that he no longer loved me. Shivani was like a newly obtained toy for him. He became obsessed with her. He started spending all his waking hours with Shivani. The minute he got back from work, he would take Shivani to the park or for a walk and I went unnoticed..."

Ragini continued, "He was not deliberately ignoring me or neglecting my presence, but for him Shivani was everything and I had moved to second place. I knew he loved me a lot but still he never showed it like he used to earlier. I started feeling lonely. I had no one to talk to, as his family and my family had both broken all connection with us."

"In my loneliness I didn't realize when I started getting close to Mithun. And as we belonged to the same community, we got along very well. Amar never minded. But I wanted him to mind. I wanted him to feel jealous."

"But Amar was very involved with Shivani and he never observed that I was getting closer than normal with Mithun who had become a regular visitor to the house."

Amartya understood that Ragini was so involved in her narration that she had forgotten to mention how Mithun was related to them. So she asked, "And Mithun was..."

Ragini said, "Oh! I am sorry doctor. Mithun was Amar's close friend and Amar trusted him a lot. Actually, Mithun was younger to me and Amar. Amar and I were almost the same age and Mithun had been Amar's junior in college. After a year or so, Mithun proposed to me. He said he loved me a lot and wanted to marry me. I did not want to leave Amar and went on refusing Mithun. But at one point of time I realized that I enjoyed spending time with Mithun who loved me more than Amar. At least that is what I felt at that time. I was young, lonely and confused. I told him I could not leave Amar and Shivani. But Mithun did not want a relationship on the sly. He said he was ready to marry me and asked me to tell Amar everything."

Ragini fell silent for a minute and then continued, "When I did actually confess, Amar was very angry. He said he would not allow me to go anywhere as I belonged to him. Somehow his behaviour put me off and I decided to leave the house and the city with Mithun. I felt like taking Shivani with me, but Mithun said it would create lot of complications. Mithun had no siblings and had lost his father very early in his life. He was worried that his mother would object. Which she did, but later on she relented."

Ragini took a deep breath and said, "My mother-in-law stayed with us until recently. She is no more now. She died of a major heart attack last September."

She continued, "I was torn between my motherly love and my own need for love from Mithun. Finally, I left the house leaving Shivani behind. When Amar filed for divorce, he got Shivani's custody. He would have taken her custody anyway. He practically lived his life for his daughter."

"I knew I would never be able to stay in the same city and not see my daughter. After the divorce we left Kolkata, never to look back. I started a new life with Mithun in Ajmer. We then moved to many other cities and finally have been in Mumbai for a while now. His work is such that we had to travel a lot. But now since he has signed a contract with a TV channel, we have settled in Mumbai."

Ragini couldn't speak. Her throat felt choked with emotion. She coughed.

Amartya got up, filled a glass of water from the jug and gave it to Ragini. The need to be loved had been so strong that Ragini had left her five-year-old daughter behind...

After drinking water, Ragini continued, "God punished me for my decision. I never conceived after that. The doctors told us that Mithun had some problem and that I would never conceive. That came as a shock for me. I requested Mithun to allow me to contact Shivani."

She wiped her tears with a handkerchief that she was clutching in her hand. In a tearful voice she continued, "But he was adamant. He clearly told me to let my past life go. He explained to me that Amar would never allow me to go anywhere near Shivani. So for the last twenty years I have been regretting leaving my daughter behind. My life has just been a routine and in the last twenty years I took care of my mother-in-law and supported Mithun in his career. I understood what I had forsaken and regretted it. I had run away for love, but I never actually found it. Mithun loves me a lot. He is very supportive and cares for me. For him I am his entire world. But I was not true to him because I missed Shivani. Probably, if I had conceived and had children I could have been busy and life wouldn't have been so lonely. I would never have forgotten Shivani though. A first born is always precious."

"I realized it too late and I have lived without her for twenty years now. I never tried to contact Shivani because Mithun had warned me to stay away from my past and also Amar loved her more. It was sensible that she grew up with her father."

Tears were flowing from Ragini's eyes. Loneliness and the realization of having made a mistake had made Ragini very emotional. Obviously, Shivani who was equally emotional had suffered a mental setback after both the men in her life had left her. Like Ragini, Shivani too had two men in her life. But who was the other man? This question troubled Amartya even more now.

"Doctor, can I see Shivani please?" asked Ragini.

She replied, "Yes, I will take you to the hospital and you can see Shivani. Please remember Ragini that Shivani is in a stupor and will not recognize you. It has been nearly two decades..."

Ragini got up and immediately opened her suitcase. "I will freshen up and get ready. Give me ten minutes doctor."

She picked a light grey and white sari from the suitcase. A photo album fell out of the suitcase. She turned around and said, "Doctor, do you want to see Shivani's pictures? I had taken this photo album with me when I had left. Not a day has gone by when I have not seen these photos. I carry it with me wherever I go."

Amartya knew now that Shivani was like Ragini in many aspects. Though Ragini had left her past behind, it was only on physical terms. Emotionally, she was still holding on to her past.

Ragini enthusiastically opened the album and showed her the pictures.

"The album has many pictures of Shivani who was around five years old at that time. There are a couple of photographs where the three of us are together and one or two photos of Amar too."

And suddenly Ragini became very sullen and said, "No one informed me when he died. I could have come here and taken Shivani with me. I curse myself for going away with Mithun. But I never realized that my poor daughter would have to grow up in a hostel. At least Mrinal *di* could have told me. But then no one knew where I was and..."

Ragini started sobbing. Amartya knew that all this might have come as a shock for Ragini. All these years wasted without a child. God can be so unforgiving at times. He had made Ragini suffer for twenty years for having left her daughter. Amartya wondered how Ragini would react when she would see Shivani.

Chapter 17

When Ragini had calmed down sufficiently and freshened up, Amartya decided to take her to the hospital to see Shivani. She picked up the album and put it in her purse. She hadn't seen the pictures. As they walked to the hospital, Ragini informed Amartya that Mithun did not know she was in Kolkata.

Ragini said, "If I had told Mithun I was coming to Kolkata, he wouldn't have allowed me to come. I told him I am going to Ajmer to attend a function. I had made some friends while I had stayed in Ajmer and I am in touch with them. I knew he wouldn't object if I went to meet them. He is very busy now with his work. Actually, I was wondering how you got my residence number."

Amartya smiled and replied, "I told you that I had gone to meet Mrs. Mrinal. She told me about Mithun Dubey being a singer and that someone had seen his performance on TV. I researched on the internet and got to know that Mithun is presently located in Mumbai. I made many telephone calls before I was able to get his residence number."

Amartya wanted to see Ragini's reaction after she saw Shivani. Though there was no chance of Shivani recognising Ragini, still Amartya felt that Ragini's presence would make a difference. It was just a gut feeling.

Somewhere deep in her heart she felt that a mother would always hold the image of her daughter close to her heart. And she had been right. Though Ragini had left Shivani, as a mother, she had placed the girl in a special place in her heart.

And as Ragini had no other children after that, Shivani was the only child she had given birth to. The feeling of motherhood would have made Ragini suffer a lot in the last twenty years. And now finally, when she had got the chance to see her daughter, it had to be in this state.

Amartya guided Ragini to her consulting room and asked the nurse to bring Shivani. Amartya opened her bag and took out the album. Shivani looked very cute. There were photographs of Shivani in her uniform, at the park playing on the swing and many others. And then Amartya saw the family photo. Amar Ghose had been a handsome man – tall, fair, a thick moustache; he was holding Shivani in his arms with Ragini on his side. A nice happy family… And then she turned the leaves of the album and saw Amar's close-up photograph which revealed his sharp features, green eyes and attractive smile. Why had Ragini left this man? He had been a loving man, good looking, financially stable… *But the human mind seeks something more than all that*, she realized.

Sister Maya brought in Shivani and seated her near Amartya's chair. Ragini sat opposite them staring at Shivani. Ragini's eyes were filled with tears and she couldn't stop looking at Shivani. She almost instinctively got up to hug Shivani. Amartya motioned her to remain seated.

"Hello Shivani, how are you feeling today? See, Shivani I know that you are hearing everything that I say and what others say, but have chosen to remain silent. Whatever the hurt whoever has caused you, it should not make you retreat from life. You must come out of this and face life head on. Nobody in our life has a right to reduce us to this state."

Shivani always either stared at the blank wall in front of her or at the table or looked down. Amartya looked at Shivani who was staring at the table. Amartya passed the glass of water to Ragini who was sobbing uncontrollably now.

Suddenly she heard Shivani scream, "He left me. He has gone away. Why did he leave me? Where has he gone?"

Amartya watched as Shivani picked up the album that was lying open on her table. Shivani caressed Amar's photograph and collapsed. Sister Maya who was standing next to Shivani's chair held Shivani and they put her on the couch.

Amar? Amar Ghose? Amartya was shocked at the revelation that Shivani had made. How was it possible? Hadn't Amar Ghose died? What had Shivani said?

Amartya waited for Shivani to gain consciousness. She looked at Ragini who was sitting dazed completely at a loss for words. And then suddenly Ragini spoke, "What is Shivani saying, doctor? Didn't Amar die? How do you know he died? Maybe he is alive or is she shocked because of her father's death? But that was many years ago. Why would she go in shock now after so many years?"

Amartya looked at Ragini who was blabbering away not at all sure of what she was speaking. Of course Amar had died. His life insurance claims etc. had been cleared. All this was not possible without proof of death. There had to be a death certificate. But all that was the practical side of the issue. If Amar was dead, who was the person who was seeing Shivani for the last so many years?

"Ragini, did Amar have a brother, a twin brother maybe?"

The minute Amartya asked the question she knew how foolish it sounded. This was getting too cinematic and unbelievable. She knew the answer even before Ragini replied.

"No doctor. He had only one sister, Mrinal *di*. Rest all are cousins."

Who was the man who had been seeing Shivani, had become her guardian angel and now disappeared leaving her like this? Only Shivani had the answer and Amartya was eager to know who he was.

Amartya could make out from Ragini's actions that she was feeling restless and fidgety. She herself was feeling the same.

Shivani woke up after a while. But her eyes were blank again, just like before. The momentary reaction had been temporary. Amartya tried to get an answer out of Shivani by asking many questions. But Shivani did not respond and remained silent and expressionless. Amartya knew that Amar's photo had triggered a reaction and wondered whether she should show Shivani the photograph again but finally decided against it.

Ragini wanted to stay in Shivani's apartment. Amartya felt it was right and called Aparna.

"Aparna, could you come to the hospital and pick up Shivani's mother? She has come from Mumbai and will be staying here for a while. Take her to Shivani's apartment and please help her settle in."

After Amartya disconnected the phone she smiled. Aparna had said that she would come in a short while to the hospital. She had been surprised to hear about Shivani's mother, about whom she had never known till now. She hadn't said anything on the phone but her tone had revealed her sentiment.

Anyway, it was good that Ragini had decided to stay at Shivani's apartment. She would feel closer to her daughter that way.

In the evening after Amartya was back at her quarters, she sat down on her favourite chair beside the window staring outside. She was thinking of Shivani's reaction. Finally, when the girl had reacted, it had been to invoke more confusion. How could Amar be seeing Shivani? There were two options. Either someone was impersonating Amar and fooling Shivani or Shivani had been imagining the whole thing. But how could Shivani imagine her dad's face when she had clearly mentioned in her diary that she did not remember her dad's or mom's face? On seeing Amar's photo she had said, 'Why did you leave me?' It indicated that the person who came to meet her looked like Amar.

He could not be Amar. How could he be Amar? How can a dead person… What was she thinking? It was all very illogical. Practically, she would have to check out if someone, probably Amar's close relative who resembled him was not playing the act and taking Shivani for a ride. But what would the other person gain by fooling Shivani? And besides, all through Shivani's life, this man had helped her and nowhere had she written a single bad trait about the person. So the person, whoever he was had behaved like a gentleman. So who was he?

This question troubled Amartya and she wondered how she was going to get her answer if Shivani remained in a trance. Should she show Shivani Amar's photo again and maybe hypnotise her? She stifled a yawn. It had been a long day. She was feeling tired and sleepy. Tomorrow she would decide on her next course of action.

Chapter 18

Amartya got up with a headache. She hadn't slept well during the night. She made a cup of strong coffee. Why was she getting so deeply involved and affected by this case? This was just a case. She felt like backing out of this case again. Was it not better to hand it over to an expert psychiatrist who was more experienced? But something inside her refused to agree.

Deep inside she knew this case was special to her. Though she was not connected to Shivani in any way, she still felt that she was the person who should take Shivani's responsibility, cure her and bring her back to normal again. Amartya knew that she would not let go of Shivani's case. If required she would seek advice from senior psychiatrists. In case she would have to hand over the case to her senior, she would still be actively involved in the case. But she had no answer for the question as to why she was holding on to Shivani or rather Shivani's case so possessively. She did not have an answer for that.

She showered and quickly got dressed. Today she would have to take some decision about Shivani. She could not let the girl just remain in a trance. The silence had to be broken.

She decided to eat breakfast at the hospital.

When she reached the hospital she met Ragini who was sitting outside in the lobby waiting for her.

"Good morning, Dr. Amartya."

"Good morning, Mrs. Ragini. Were you able to settle in comfortably at Shivani's apartment yesterday?"

"Yes, doctor. Aparna took me there and she called a maid to get the house cleaned. She also helped me bring in the required groceries and all for cooking. She is a nice girl. She was telling me many things about Shivani. She was happy to see me."

"That is good. So that indicates you are planning to stay longer."

"Yes, I am planning to stay for two weeks as of now. I managed to convince Mithun and as he is busy with the latest television series, he doesn't mind my absence. He doesn't know that I am in Kolkata. Doctor, when will Shivani speak? Why is she not speaking? I can't see a single emotion in her eyes. I am seeing my daughter after so many years and she is in this state."

Amartya saw Ragini sniffing, holding back tears. This woman was a mystery. In the first place she left her daughter for another man and then even after twenty years she still was getting so emotional for her daughter. Was this how mothers felt? She remembered her mother's words – '*A mother stays connected to her child at all times even after she severs the umbilical cord and separates the child from her at birth.*' Amartya felt tears stinging her eyes. She had lost the chance of becoming a mother and lost her own mother too...

She decided to go to Shivani's room instead of bringing the girl to the consulting room. She had to get on with the case. She had to concentrate on her work. This was no time for her personal tragedies to surface.

"Mrs. Ragini, do you want to come with me to Shivani's room? We will go and check how she is today."

"Yes, I would like to see her again. But I had some doubts. Doctor, is there any chance of Amar being alive? If not, was Shivani seeing someone who looked like Amar? If so, who was he and where is he now?"

Amartya decided to tell Ragini about the diaries and all that she had read about the man.

"Sit down, Mrs. Ragini. I think it is time to tell you something."

After Amartya finished telling about the diary entries and about the man in Shivani's life, Ragini was shocked and asked, "Could he have harmed my Shivani? It couldn't be Amar. He is no more. Right doctor?"

"Yes Mrs. Ragini, Amar is no more. Mrs. Mrinal told me that she deposited all the insurance money and other savings in a trust for Shivani. So surely, Amar is no more. Still, to be absolutely sure on this, I will call up and check out Amar's death certificate. His accident happened in Kolkata and some hospital surely issued the death certificate. By tomorrow we will know the details. Come, let us go and see Shivani."

Amartya entered Shivani's room. Ragini stood at the entrance with a sad look on her face. Shivani was sitting upright with the pillow supporting her back and was staring at the wall.

"Hello Shivani, how are you feeling today?"

Amartya checked her pulse. Everything was normal. But the girl just stared at the blank wall not responding. Amartya wondered if Amar's photograph would bring out another reaction from Shivani. She decided to try. She knew if it didn't work, she would have to hypnotise her patient. She asked the nurse to get the album from her desk.

Ragini entered the room and stood in a corner silently not sure what to do. Amartya knew that Ragini was afraid, afraid that when Shivani will speak and respond, she will get angry on seeing her mother who had come to show sympathy after so many years. She might even ask her to go back and not want to see her again. All these fears were visible in Ragini's eyes. Amartya checked Shivani's eyes. They were blank, no expression at all. She had gone back into her shell again.

Amartya took the photo album from Sister Maya. She took Amar's photo and held it in front of Shivani. She hoped Shivani would react in some way, say something...

But the girl did not react at all. She did not even look at the photograph. She just stared through everything. She would have to hypnotise the girl. She would speak up when hypnotised. Only doubt that Amartya had was, whether the girl would reveal anything other than what she had penned in her diary. If she spoke about what she had already written in the diary, it would be of no help.

There had to be some other information, something about the man that Shivani had not written but had stored in her subconscious mind and would reveal when hypnotised.

As soon as they stepped out of the room, Ragini started sobbing. She asked, "What has happened to her, doctor? Why is Shivani not speaking? Yesterday after seeing Amar's photograph she had spoken. But today she is not reacting at all. Will she ever be cured?"

"Of course, Shivani will be fine soon. Mrs. Ragini, please do not think negatively and do not worry. As of now the case is in my hand. I have taken all the steps required to understand Shivani's silence. Now I know what treatment I can start on her. I will also seek advice on her case from senior psychiatrists who are more experienced. They would definitely have the answers. She is going to be normal again."

After Ragini left, Amartya made some enquiries about Amar and by evening found out that Amar Ghose had died on the spot in a ghastly accident on 4th Main, Circle Street. The Holy Spirit Hospital had issued the death certificate. Amar had died. So it was not Amar that Shivani was seeing. Then who was that man? Why had Shivani seen Amar's photo and reacted?

Would Mrs. Mrinal help in finding out if any of the relatives resembled Amar? Amartya called up Mrs. Mrinal and spoke to her. The information she received was negative. None of the relatives even slightly resembled Amar. She had said that Amar was special in his own way and none of their cousins or in fact even she herself had not been blessed with sharp features and green eyes like Amar's.

Amartya felt like she had reached the dead end. If Amar was no more, and no relatives looked like him, then who was this man Shivani had been seeing. Amartya recalled yesterday's scene when Shivani had seen Amar's photo on her desk and screamed. So it was Amar who visited her. There was no other man like him. So it had to be him. How?

It was practically impossible that Amar had been visiting Shivani and so it meant that Shivani had been imagining the whole thing. For so many years the girl had been imagining that a man was helping her. It all seemed quite impossible and unbelievable. Was Shivani schizophrenic? Instead of wasting time in trying to analyze her doubts, she decided to speak to her senior, Dr. Maniyar who had more than thirty years experience and had handled many complicated cases. She called his clinic and fixed up an appointment with him for next morning.

She was feeling tensed. The case was getting very complicated and confusing. She needed some information, an important clue or a missing link to understand Shivani's silence. Tomorrow she would meet Dr. Maniyar and hopefully he would be able to help her...

Chapter 19

Amartya sat outside Dr Maniyar's room. She had an appointment with him at 10 a.m. She had reached a good fifteen minutes early. She looked around the reception area and saw the receptionist busy fixing appointments on the phone. There were so many people who needed psychiatric help. It was really sad. When she had chosen this field, she had known she would meet many different kinds of patients with varied mental problems. But this profession had always fascinated her. The human mind and its complications had attracted her. She knew that the physical body was just like a piece of machinery. It was the mind which was powerful and which had the control radars of the body parts. Curing a physical illness never interested her. The human mind was the crux of all ailments and that was why she had chosen Psychiatry. Unravelling the mysteries of the mind was what interested her. Now in Shivani's case also, she wondered what had gone wrong in the girl's mind which had created a self imposed silence and withdrawal. Mental traumas never happen suddenly. The link is always and always something from the past…

"Dr. Amartya, you may go in now. Dr. Maniyar is waiting for you," said the girl at the reception.

Amartya got up and knocked the door lightly before entering Dr. Maniyar's room.

"Hello Amartya, it's been a long time now since I saw you. How are you?"

Amartya smiled. Dr. Maniyar looked the same. She had last seen him a couple of years ago at a seminar.

He was the same smiling old gentleman. He was short, heavily built and bald. Yet, he looked quite young for his fifty plus age.

His smile was what attracted her. Probably his patients too felt reassured when he smiled. He had a very positive attitude and was always smiling.

"Hello, Dr. Maniyar. It is always a pleasure to meet you. I will not waste much of your time as I know you are busy with your patients during this time of the morning. I am caught in a case where I needed your help urgently. I will come straight to the point. It is about my patient Shivani Ghose."

Amartya narrated everything she knew about Shivani till date and included her conclusions too. Dr. Maniyar listened patiently absorbing every word that she had spoken.

At the end, Amartya sighed and leaned forward waiting for his response. She looked eagerly at Dr. Maniyar and hoped that he would be able to clear some of her doubts.

"How is it possible that the girl is seeing this dead man, her dead father, doctor?" she asked.

"See Amartya, this is not a regular case. This girl has been seeing her father who is actually dead. There are a couple of ways to look at this. One, that the girl is imagining the whole thing. The existence of this man, his assurances, everything that you said now… That would explain why she has not written any description at all. But this would mean a very complicated mental disequilibrium. Another is that though Amar Ghose left his body during the accident, his soul is still around. Or at least was around till the time Shivani saw him. Now…"

"But Dr. Maniyar that is not possible. I know about souls and all. The soul leaves the body when the person dies and enters another body. But we can't obviously see souls."

Dr. Maniyar said, "Shivani has never seen the soul. The logical explanation is that Amar's soul spoke to Shivani but it had no form. The form or rather the face was always in Shivani's subconscious mind."

"But she has written in her diary that she doesn't remember her father's face."

"So? Amartya you have drifted on this one. The subconscious mind stores all the images. Yes, technically she doesn't remember her father's face. But it was her father with whom she lived till she was eight. Obviously the image of his face is imprinted in her memory. But when he died and left her, she pushed the image into the deep recesses of her mind."

"When you look at her, what do you feel Amartya? Does she look like she has lost it? Or does her face look calm and undeterred?"

Amartya closed her eyes for a moment and visualised Shivani.

"Shivani does not look like she is a mental case or something. It just looks like she has voluntarily or rather involuntarily decided to shut down."

Dr. Maniyar rubbed his stubble and thought for a minute before saying, "So then, it is the second evaluation which is correct. Amar's soul never took another body because when he died he knew he had left many responsibilities behind. He could not die. He did not want to die. He stayed on till Shivani got engaged and when he felt that his daughter was in safe hands, he decided to move on."

Amartya leaned back on the chair and sighed. Somehow she was not quite convinced. Instinctively she knew that Dr. Maniyar couldn't be wrong. But she couldn't make herself believe about souls and all. It was not logical at all. But was the mind logical? Maybe not. But souls and all? She was finding it difficult to trust Dr. Maniyar's judgement.

Dr. Maniyar as though guessing her thoughts said, "See Amartya, I know this is not easy for you. But I have read very much in detail on this topic. In fact I am glad you came to me. There is a lot of research going on about the innumerable lives of a soul and past life regression in our field. Haven't you read the latest research work by Dr. Louis David? You must read it. Rather, I will suggest that you attend the seminar on this subject to be held next week in Chennai. The seminar is 'by invitation only' and I will arrange for an invitation in your name. I am going there and you can accompany me."

Amartya had her own doubts. She asked, "Doctor, is there life after life? I mean, don't we actually die? Don't we burn or bury the body and is that not the end of life? Okay, we are reborn and take up another body but doesn't our existence end when we first die? Don't we start a new life, a new existence with a new entity after we die? Do we have a choice of not taking another body? Isn't it sort of automatic that we enter another body as soon as we leave one body? This is all very confusing and actually as you say, I should learn more about it. I will attend the seminar in Chennai next week."

"See Amartya, whether it is life or human mind… it is not as stable or as simple as we think it is. There is a lot more. There is a universal power which rules the universe and all the happenings in it."

He continued, "How far our medical research has reached, there is still a lot left to research and unveil. In this seminar, a Swamiji is going to speak on 'life after death' and 're-birth'. He is very knowledgeable on this subject and I think he will be able to guide you."

Amartya felt shocked to hear about Swamis and all and said, "Dr. Maniyar. Please don't tell me that some Swamiji can tell us what to do in our field. You are such an experienced psychiatrist and there are so many others in our field. How can an uneducated person or at least a person who has no knowledge about our field speak to us on psychiatry or guide us? How would he know about re-birth or soul for that matter? He would mainly speak about God and the powers of God."

Dr. Maniyar smiled and said, "Amartya, we have learnt a lot about our field from books, experiences and research. But yet, when it comes to souls or something that we can't prove physically, we are at a loss. Aren't we? This Swamiji is a great saint who has meditated in the Himalayas. I have heard about him from my colleagues and they say he has immense knowledge on the subject of souls. Yes, he is not educated in our field. But it seems whatever he speaks makes sense. And he is ready to prove it. He is going to speak on past lives and the universal cosmic energy."

"Many psychiatrists try past life regression or hypnotic regression on patients where they can take the patient hundreds or thousands of years into their past. The patient then speaks of his past lives, his roles and some other memories. You know about this, don't you?"

"Yes Dr. Maniyar, I have heard of it. But I have never approved of it. I mean what is the whole point in this regression. It is with great difficulty that we are able to sort out our issues in our current life. I always believe it is better to stay in the present and sort out the existing mental traumas."

"Amartya, we all wish it was that way."

He sighed and said, "Anyway, I think that even if you hypnotise Shivani, she will not reveal anything new. Nothing that you don't know..."

He continued, "You found her diaries locked in a bookshelf. What does it indicate about her nature? That she preferred privacy and did not want people to know what she wrote in her diary or the fact that she wrote a diary. Similarly, there were certain things that she did not even write in her diary. Isn't it? So these emotions or thoughts were locked away somewhere deep inside her mind. Even if you hypnotise her, there is very little hope of her revealing much about this man she saw. We know from her outburst that it was Amar. So we go on ahead knowing that Amar died, his soul left his body but never entered another body. He spoke to Shivani and helped her sort all her issues. Souls don't have a form. They are just energy. But then what are we made up of? We are energy too.

So communication occurs. You come to this seminar and you will meet many experienced doctors from all over the world. You can discuss your case or listen to their experiences, their case histories and evaluate your case better."

Amartya knew that she was left with no choice. Attending the seminar would mean learning about the latest research in their field and meeting experienced doctors. The seminar would mean moving one step ahead in her career. But she was not sure about Swamiji. She decided to take leave of Dr. Maniyar.

"Thank you Dr. Maniyar. I trust your guidance and will proceed with my treatment keeping in mind the advice you have given me. I need to think, rethink on all the aspects of life and death that you have spoken about. I will see you at the seminar in Chennai."

Chapter 20

Amartya walked out of the clinic and waved a cab. There was a lot of traffic today. The cab was moving at a snail's pace. The honking of the cars and buses did not bother her. She was lost in her own world thinking about all that Dr. Maniyar had told her.

How could a soul talk or communicate? Had the girl held onto her father's image? Had she imagined that her father was coming to meet her? Or was it that Amar's soul had stayed on and helped Shivani? She knew Ragini would call her to ask if there was any progress in Shivani's case. What would she tell her?

Should she hypnotise Shivani and find out more about Amar's appearance in her life. But like Dr. Maniyar had said, probably Shivani had locked away that part of her life and wouldn't speak even when hypnotised. She might just say the things that she had already penned in her diary. Or she might not. She would have to find out.

Her cell phone rang and she knew it would be Ragini wanting to know about her discussion with Dr. Maniyar.

"Hello doctor, Ragini here. Did you meet Dr. Maniyar? Will he be guiding you in Shivani's treatment?"

"Hello, yes Mrs. Ragini, I met him. I am in the cab now on my way back to the hospital. I can't speak to you now. I will speak to you later. Are you coming to the hospital to see Shivani?"

"Yes doctor, I will leave now and wait for you at the hospital" said Ragini.

She decided not to tell Ragini anything about Dr. Maniyar's deductions. If she told her about Amar's soul interacting with Shivani, Ragini would be scared. It was more practical to tell her about the seminar she would be attending. She could reassure Ragini by saying that she would be meeting a lot of experienced doctors who would be able to shed more light in Shivani's case.

Amartya stared out of the cab. She thought, 'Wouldn't it be better if Shivani was sent home and taken care of by Ragini?'

A full time nurse could be appointed. As Shivani did not react violently or have outbursts, she could be sent home provided there was someone to take care of her 24/7. Probably that would rekindle her emotions and she might feel like living her life again. It was better than keeping her here at the hospital where she safely went into her haven of silence and did not have the urge to react or feel. In her own house maybe she would look around, see her things and feel secure. But this was possible only if Ragini was ready to stay back and take Shivani's responsibility. She would have to speak to Ragini and confirm with her before taking the decision of discharging Shivani from the hospital.

Amartya went directly to the Dean's office and spoke to him about Shivani's case.

The Dean said, "You are right Dr. Amartya. If there is someone to take care of the girl, it is better to send her home."

"Sir, I am planning to attend the seminar at Chennai with Dr. Maniyar."

"That is good news, Amartya. Some of my colleagues are attending the seminar."

The Dean continued, "Not all doctors have been invited for the seminar. You are lucky that Dr. Maniyar is taking you along with him. Very limited passes have been issued. Did you know the seminar is titled 'Life after death'?"

"Dr. Maniyar did not tell me that. But he did inform me about the topics that were going to be discussed," replied Amartya.

Amartya took leave of the Dean and decided to start the discharge procedure if Ragini agreed to take care of Shivani.

When Amartya walked towards her consulting room, she saw Ragini seated outside, waiting for her.

"Hello, Mrs. Ragini."

"Hello, doctor. I wanted to see Shivani once more. I was hoping to go along with you when you go on your daily rounds. Is that okay? And doctor, if you don't mind could you just call me Ragini? Somehow Mrs. Ragini sounds too formal," Ragini requested.

"That is fine. You can accompany me when I go to see Shivani. Come inside and take a seat Ragini. I want to speak to you," said Amartya.

After Ragini was seated comfortably Amartya continued, "I want to know how long you plan to stay here in Kolkata."

Ragini thought for a minute before replying, "I cannot stay for more than a couple of weeks, doctor. Mithun will be curious and he might get angry. I have never stayed away so long. He will not like it."

"Oh! I was hoping that you could stay longer and take care of Shivani at her home. As she is not a reactive patient, she could be sent home and brought in at intervals for treatment. But if you are not planning to stay longer and as there is no one else to take care of Shivani, it is better she stays here at the hospital. I had actually consulted the Dean about this and he too opined that Shivani could be sent home," said Amartya disappointedly.

Ragini was quiet for a while. Amartya wondered what was going on in Ragini's mind. As far as she could judge, a mother's heart would win over a wife's heart.

"Doctor, please give me a day to sort this out. I really want to stay back and take care of Shivani. She is my daughter and I have left her alone for just too long. Now when I have the opportunity, I want to take care of her. I will speak to Mithun and try to convince him. I am sure he will understand."

Amartya was glad that the mother in Ragini had won. It looked like this time she was not going to make the mistake of leaving her daughter.

"Ragini, I am going to Chennai to attend a seminar. Dr. Maniyar invited me and in this seminar I will be meeting many expert psychiatrists and I am sure I will be able to get the answer to Shivani's problem."

"Doctor, I have been wondering how Amar had been seeing Shivani? I mean, a ghost or..."

Amartya smiled as Ragini left her sentence incomplete.

"There are no ghosts, Ragini. Stop worrying about such things. I have spoken to Dr. Maniyar who is an experienced psychiatrist and he is sure that I will be getting very good advice at the seminar. By next week, I am sure I would have all the answers and we could immediately start the right treatment on Shivani. As of now, whatever we do, no medicines or anything can make her talk. She doesn't want to speak. It is not a conscious decision. If she would have lost her voice due to some trauma, we could have easily treated her. But she has lost interest in life. It is like slow suicide. She doesn't want to live and so does not acknowledge anything that is around her. She is like that tortoise who has gone into the shell. We can't see anything except the hard cover."

She continued, "See Ragini, we can give shock treatment to bring her out of shock. But I do not recommend shock treatments. It is not advisable at this stage. I want to know what exactly transpired in her mind, why she decided to be silent and what or who can make her want to live life again. I can show her Amar's photograph and then hypnotise her and find out more about what had happened. As of now, she is fine the way she is. I prefer she is taken home so that she can be in her own environment which will help her come to terms with life. She needs to be in a familiar place. You could appoint a nurse to take care of her and you could check on her all the time. This is to ensure that she is safe and doesn't decide to do something reckless. But I doubt she will do anything like that."

Amartya looked at Ragini who had been listening intently. Now it was Ragini's choice if she wanted to take care of her daughter or not. Either way, her patient was more important. If Ragini was unable to take care of Shivani, it was better she stayed at the hospital.

She sat patiently waiting for Ragini to speak up.

Ragini was staring at the paper weight on the table. She picked it up and turned it round and round. After a few minutes she said, "I will call Mithun today and convince him. Either way I don't care.

I want to take care of my Shivani and I am going to do it. Nobody can stop me from taking care of my own daughter."

Though it was quite an outburst, there was conviction in her tone and Amartya appreciated it. The woman was not actually afraid of anything. She had guts. She could take any decision she wanted to and implement it once she made up her mind. Amartya deducted that as long as Ragini had felt that Amar was there to take care of Shivani, she had never interfered. But now when she knew that her daughter was alone and needed her, she would not back out.

Finally, a mother is always a mother. Amartya felt a strange emotion rise inside her. She missed her mom. A major heart attack had taken her mom away from her. With great effort she brought herself out of her past. Why was she drifting to her past so often nowadays? She had to treat Shivani and make her normal again. It was important for her to help Shivani. It was a professional challenge.

But somehow this case was bringing out the personal issues of her past. There was no point in dwelling in her past. Some of the memories were very painful. 'But the mind always keeps the painful memories on the top shelf for easy perusal at all times,' she thought cynically.

She reprimanded herself for thinking of her past. This was not the time. She looked at Ragini who was sitting lost in thoughts. Maybe Ragini was still feeling guilty about her past. Ragini suddenly came out of her stupor and said, "Doctor, I have made my decision. I will take Shivani home. You are right. She will feel better if she stays in familiar surroundings. I will also ask Aparna to drop in once in a while and try to make everything as normal as possible. Kindly go ahead with the discharge formalities as soon as you can. I am ready to take full responsibility of my daughter till she is perfectly alright and even later. That is, if she wants me."

Amartya was surprised with Ragini's sudden decision.

"See Ragini, please think once more before taking this decision. Once you take Shivani home, she will get used to having you around. Even if she doesn't speak, she will start acknowledging things and people in the house. She might also decide to break her silence once she knows you are a permanent factor in her life. She could tell you things, or share her feelings. And after that if you leave her, she will not be able to bear the shock. So be very sure of your decision. This whole thing might take more than six months, even a year maybe. But I am sure that once Shivani sees you around daily, day in and day out, her silence will falter. The urge to speak out will get stronger within her. Be patient with her and love her."

"Whoever the person she had been seeing had given her a sense of security and you too need to do that. You have to be able to give her so much peace, love and security that she will feel safe again. Do you think you can do that?" asked Amartya.

Ragini had tears in her eyes but Amartya saw the firm determination and strength in her eyes. Shivani needed love and security and now Ragini had the chance to give that. There was no way Ragini was going to miss the chance again.

"Doctor, I am willing to take up full responsibility. She is my daughter, my only child and I will do anything for her. I have wasted too many years and now I will make up for that. I assure you I will not leave her and go."

Amartya just hoped that Shivani would come out of her trance once she returned home. But that still would not solve the case. Who was the man? If it was Amar or his soul like Dr. Maniyar had said, where was the soul now? How could a soul take a form or speak? All this was way beyond her understanding. If Shivani became normal and spoke about the man, she would still miss him if he didn't reappear. That part of her life had to be resolved.

She decided to start the discharge formalities immediately. Ragini would have to sign the documents before taking Shivani home. Tomorrow Ragini could take Shivani home. Amartya decided to hypnotise Shivani and see if she revealed anything new.

After Ragini left, she called Sister Maya and asked her to bring Shivani. Sister Maya brought in Shivani who just stared at the wall. Her eyes were blank. Amartya closed the door, checked if Shivani was sitting comfortably and started her treatment. She was going to hypnotise Shivani and see if she revealed anything.

"Click," she snapped her fingers.

"Shivani, Shivani how are you feeling?"

Shivani opened her eyes and again just stared at the wall.

Well, at least she had revealed something under hypnosis, sighed Amartya.

After Shivani was taken back to the room, Amartya leaned back on her chair and closed her eyes. Shivani had spoken about some of the incidents that she had written in the diary. Most of it she had read. She had spoken about school, college and her office. Then she had spoken about Arun. The girl really loved him. But she had spoken a lot about Amar also. Again she had not described his appearance. She had said that her guardian angel was a good looking man in his mid thirty's. He was kind, loving and caring. He never hurt her, he spoke very softly.

Amartya recalled asking what she would do if her guardian angel didn't come at all. Shivani had suddenly become silent and then had sobbed for a couple of minutes. After which she had said, "I can't live without him. He has to be there with me to guide me, help me take decisions and stand by me. I need his support. I feel very insecure without him."

The way Shivani had described her guardian angel matched Amar's characteristics. But how was that possible? Dr. Maniyar's words rung inside her head. A soul? With a form? It was impossible. Amar's soul would have taken another body many years ago and might be living comfortably somewhere in some part of the world.

Maybe Shivani was imagining the whole thing. Amar's coming, helping her; everything was probably just an illusion. Whatever it was, she had to sort it out for Shivani. The seminar would help her come to a right conclusion. She truly hoped so....

Chapter 21

Amartya sat in the airplane. The seat next to her was unoccupied. Dr. Maniyar had called her in the morning informing her of his change in plans. His wife was sick and had been hospitalized and he was not joining her for the seminar. She was going alone. Dr. Maniyar's presence would have made a difference in the sense that he would have known many other experts at the seminar and she would have got an easy introduction. He had given her the names and references of a couple of doctors attending the seminar. She could meet them and speak to them about her case.

Amartya realized that she had been too involved in routine cases to have delved deeper into the latest research on souls and other related topics. She had been a good student at the university and had scored well. But that had all been book knowledge. She had encountered various types of cases during the last ten years. But none had been like Shivani's case and so she had been able to tackle them quite easily. She had basked in her success and not bothered to move on and take more complicated cases.

It was only when the plane landed with a mild thud that she woke up. She came out of the airport carrying her small overnight bag. The climate was very hot and humid in Chennai. She had never come here before. She took a cab to the Royal Sheraton Hotel, the venue for the seminar. All the doctors attending the seminar were booked in the same hotel. She paid the cab driver and entered the hotel.

There was quite a crowd in the lobby. She assumed that most of them were doctors. The receptionist told her that the entire hotel had been booked for the seminar.

She freshened up and checked the schedules for the discussion. The first round was to begin at 11 a.m. She decided to wear a white sari with a red and gold border. At 10.55 a.m. she walked out of her room towards the conference hall.

There was lot of hustle bustle outside the conference room. She went inside and took the seat allotted to her. The conference room was more like a hall and systematic seating had been arranged for more than hundred doctors. Everyone was discussing about Swamiji. She overheard someone say that his name was Swami Shripathi but that every one preferred to call him Swamiji. Suddenly there was a hush hush silence and she turned around to see an old man walking across the room. Two doctors escorted him to the podium. He was wearing saffron robes, was of medium height, thin, with grey hair and a long white beard. She couldn't make out his age. He did not have any wrinkles on his face. As she was sitting in the front row, she could see him clearly. He held his back straight as he walked slowly and confidently to his seat. His grey hair indicated that he was old, maybe sixty plus or so, guessed Amartya. She waited for Swamiji to speak as she wanted to know what he would say that the expert doctors or research scientists did not know about.

The discussion started with a basic introduction speech by Dr. Jeff Harris, one of the leading doctors of America. After he sat down, Swamiji smiled and began speaking.

Amartya listened with rapt attention to his godly voice. His smile had changed the energy in the room. It was as though suddenly extra lights had been switched on. There was something very special about Swamiji. Was it his voice? Everybody in the room was listening intently and there was total silence.

When Swamiji finished speaking he asked all the doctors if they had any questions or doubts. Several doctors asked various questions on the entity of the soul, about life after death, and whether souls die. Swamiji had ready answers to all the questions. He never faltered even once. In fact, he cracked jokes and explained everything quite easily. Amartya sat silently listening to everyone.

There was a break for lunch after which the discussion would continue at 4 p.m. She was not feeling hungry. A huge buffet spread had been arranged. There were many varieties of Indian curries, rice and some meat, fish and breads which looked suitable for the American palate. She did not feel like eating anything. She finally picked up a sandwich and went to her room. She wanted to sit for a while and think about what Swamiji had spoken.

He had said that it is the body that dies and the soul never dies. So what happens to the soul? The soul is reincarnated as it takes another body, or rather enters another body. So what about God? Wasn't God up there governing the whole thing? Who was this supreme power? The topic for discussion in the evening was 'past life regression' and she was not sure she wanted to attend it. What was the point anyway in going into the past lives and finding out what or who we were?

But by quarter to four, she changed her mind and decided to go. She changed into a lemon yellow kurta and white trouser and wrapped a red and yellow stole around her neck. There was no point in sitting inside the hotel room. She had come here to learn about the latest research in her field. Also she wanted to listen to what Swamiji would say. She wanted to know more about him and how he was able to speak so much on science.

She stepped inside the lift. The conference hall was on the first floor. She felt pulled towards the conference room. She settled down in the front row. She stared at the large red chair where Swamiji had been sitting a while ago. How had he gathered so much knowledge? She wanted to speak to Swamiji personally. Though she had so many doubts about Swamiji's source of knowledge, she felt drawn to his voice and words. There was truth and conviction in his words...

The discussion was marvellous. Many of the doctors had thrown out several questions and Swamiji had just sat there with a calm and serene look on his face answering all the questions totally unperturbed. At the end of the session, Dr. Harris announced that tomorrow Swamiji would be meeting the doctors personally and anyone who wished to meet him could fix up an appointment.

Amartya was glad that she would get to speak to Swamiji in privacy. She wanted to ask about Shivani's case but not in front of all the other doctors. She fixed an appointment with him for 3 p.m.

She wanted to understand what it was about this 'Godman' that attracted all the doctors and scores of people in the country. At night she researched information about him on the internet and did not find a single negative story on him. When doctors became helpless and couldn't help their patients, this saint was able to help them. How was he doing it? There were certain cases where doctors couldn't help the patient beyond a certain point. And that is when they would say – 'Only a miracle can cure you now. Start offering prayers to the Almighty'. And people turned to Swamiji for help and were cured.

Swamiji did not seem to be very well educated; he did not even speak very good English. He had said that he had done lot of *sadhana* (penance) in the Himalayas and had received all the answers from God himself. Amartya was not convinced. She couldn't believe it… She would find out more about him tomorrow afternoon when she met him.

She slept off around 10 p.m. and woke up at 8 a.m. She was feeling hungry. After taking bath she picked up the phone and dialled room service. She ordered toast, orange marmalade, fresh fruit slices and a cup of coffee. After eating she decided to talk to the doctors referred by Dr. Maniyar.

She saw that most of the doctors were relaxing in the lounge. Many of them were waiting for their appointment with Swamiji. She asked for Dr. Jain and learnt that he was with Dr. Rizwan at the restaurant. Amartya went to the restaurant to meet them. Dr. Maniyar had told her to discuss her case with them. She saw the two of them seated in a corner discussing something intensely.

She guessed it was Dr. Jain as per the description given to her by Dr. Maniyar.

"Dr. Jain? I am Amartya John. Dr. Maniyar…"

Even before she could complete her sentence, Dr. Jain got up from his seat and shook hands with her.

"Hello, Dr. Amartya. This is Dr. Rizwan. He is an expert psychiatrist and has handled very complicated cases in his career. Dr. Maniyar is a very good friend of ours. He was supposed to come for the seminar. But I didn't see him yesterday."

Amartya took in Dr. Jain's appearance. He was not very tall, medium height, middle aged, fair and bald. He peered through his spectacles when he spoke. He had intelligent eyes.

She pulled a chair and joined them. They had finished eating and were drinking coffee. Dr. Rizwan ordered coffee for her He had very small eyes, was dark complexioned, wore spectacles. He spoke softly, his voice just barely louder than a whisper.

She said, "Dr. Maniyar's wife is not keeping well, so he was unable to make it to the seminar."

Dr. Jain said, "He had called up last week and informed me that you would be here at the seminar and that you wanted to discuss a case of yours."

Amartya told them about Shivani. She did not leave out anything and told them everything including the diary entries and her reaction on seeing Amar's photograph.

Dr. Jain and Dr. Rizwan discussed the case asking her about Shivani's behavioural pattern and her speech under hypnosis. Their deductions matched Dr. Maniyar's and Amartya was slightly disappointed.

She thanked both the doctors for their guidance and walked out of the restaurant. If all the experts in her field had similar deductions, why was she not convinced? Why was she not able to believe in what they were saying?

She walked into the lounge area and sat near the fountain. There were many doctors sitting in groups discussing loudly about the latest findings, research and the book by Dr. David. She sat there thinking about Shivani. Who was that man who had been seeing Shivani? She couldn't believe that souls existed outside the body and could communicate. It sounded too impractical.

Chapter 22

It was nearing lunch time. She decided to eat something and freshen up before meeting Swamiji. She had a quick lunch of penne pasta. It was deliciously made in a combination of tomato and cheese sauce, topped with fresh basil leaves and black olives with a drizzle of olive oil. She did not want to be late for her appointment with Swamiji.

She went to her room and splashed water on her face. She wiped her face and combed her hair. Should she tell everything about Shivani to Swamiji? Would he be able to guide her? She had already spoken to three experts in her field and was disappointed with their answers. What was she expecting from Swamiji? What would he know about psychiatry? Why was she going to meet him? She had no answers. She was just feeling that pull. Her instincts told her that she had to meet Swamiji and speak to him. She shrugged, picked her purse and locked the room.

There was quite a crowd outside Swamiji's room. She entered the room. There was a young boy who guided her inside. As soon as she entered Swamiji's room, she could sense a strange positive energy – the beautiful aroma of incense sticks and flowers floated in the room. She closed her eyes for a moment and sighed. She was feeling relaxed. She hadn't realized that she had been tensed.

"Hello, Dr. Amartya. How can I help you?" asked Swamiji in his soft and stable voice.

"I had some questions and some…."

"Doubts?" asked Swamiji even before Amartya could complete her sentence.

"Ask what you want to ask," he said with a serene smile on his face. Amartya sat down cross-legged on the floor. She looked at Swamiji. He looked so peaceful.

"Swamiji, I am a psychiatrist and I have a patient who has retreated into a shell and refuses to speak. She does not want to live and was admitted in a case of suicidal depression. She had been interacting with a man for the last ten years or so. Some research on her past and her one time reaction after seeing her father's photograph reveals that she had been interacting with a soul, actually her father's soul. I wanted to know how this was possible. I always believed that when the soul leaves the body, it enters another body. I mean, the journey of the soul is over when it leaves a particular body. How can a soul linger around and talk or take a form, a human form? I came to the conclusion that my patient had been imagining a person all the while and that she actually never communicated with any person. But I was not happy with my conclusion and sought advice from some expert psychiatrists who told me that Shivani was indeed interacting with her father's soul. I find it impossible to believe."

Amartya stopped herself. What was she talking? She had just blabbered away everything that had come on her mind. Where were her presentation skills? She always spoke clearly and presented her facts in the right order. But Swamiji sat silently listening to her, not bothered by her outburst. He sat silently for a few minutes and then he spoke.

"Child, let me clear your biggest doubt first. Your patient had actually been interacting with her father's soul. This is not imagination. It is the truth. And another thing is the journey of a soul doesn't actually end with one body. Scientists are researching on this."

"But how is it possible Swamiji? Her father died long ago. Does it mean his soul was still around and talking to her? I just can't believe this. And after the girl got engaged and was to marry, the soul disappeared. Now she is in a mess. How could she have seen a soul? It is all so implausible and unrealistic."

"It might certainly seem unrealistic from the eyes of a doctor, but believe me dear child, it is the truth. There is so much you need to know. Your journey has not even begun."

Amartya sat quietly lost in thoughts. What did he mean by '*journey not begun*'? She had been married once. She was a practicing psychiatrist with a good record of having treated many patients. Her journey had begun long ago.

"You need to know more about life and life after death. The seminar is over and there will not be any more discussions. I will be leaving in the evening for my ashram. In case you want to start your journey homewards and want peace with yourself, you are welcome to visit the ashram. For the next few months I will be staying at the ashram after which I will be visiting some countries to attend seminars. Many people come and meet me there. Every evening I give *diksha* (lessons) on life, soul, death and beyond."

Amartya knew that the discussion had ended. She thanked Swamiji who blessed her and she returned to her room to pack. She too was leaving by the evening flight and had to finish her check out formalities at the hotel. She had come to the seminar to seek answers. The answers she had received were not in the least satisfactory.

Each of the doctors had suggested regular hypnosis sessions which would slowly reveal the mental instabilities of the patient and bring her out of the shell of silence. And all of them believed that Shivani had been interacting with Amar's soul.

The doctors had been so interested in discussing about life after death, the karmic philosophy etc. What were they all getting involved in? What would happen in their field if all the doctors took to spirituality? Would it mean that when they failed in their treatments, instead of looking to the research department for help, they would just send their patients to ashrams and swamis?

She was feeling quite low when she boarded the flight back to Kolkata. She was feeling helpless. She settled down in her seat and as the flight took off she closed her eyes.

Swamiji's tranquil face flashed before her. He was smiling. *Journey homewards...* What had he meant by that? Wasn't she on her journey home now, to Kolkata? She recollected seeing something in his eyes. As though he had seen her past and knew all that she had been through. Was it possible? Swamiji possessed extremely good sixth sense. His words played like a cassette in her mind. On and on, rewind and again play. She was jolted out of her reverie when the flight landed. She had spent the entire journey recollecting Swamiji's words.

She took her bag and walked out of the airport and waved a cab. She was feeling drained and tired. She never felt like this. Was it the air travel that was making her feel sick? Why was she feeling so drained?

She knew that tomorrow the Dean would call her to ask about the seminar. But for now she just wanted to sleep. She took a quick shower and had a glass of milk. She was not feeling hungry. So she decided to skip dinner. She rearranged the bedcovers before lying down on the bed. She then closed her eyes wanting to fall asleep instantly. But it was a futile attempt. Sleep evaded her. As soon as she closed her eyes, Swamiji's face appeared. What was happening to her? Was she going crazy or what? And suddenly it dawned on her that he had spoken to her about her journey. But she had been sitting there and speaking about Shivani. Why then had Swamiji spoken about her and not Shivani?

She decided to recollect word to word whatever Swamiji had spoken. He had said that she was not in peace with herself. Not exactly in that way, but something like *'in case you want to begin your journey homewards and want peace with yourself'*. What had he meant by that? Of course she was peaceful. She was totally at peace with herself. She was happy and content. Or wasn't she?

Suddenly she jumped up from her bed and started pacing the room. Wasn't she happy with her life? She realized that Swamiji had spoken the absolute truth. Somewhere deep inside her there was this turmoil of the disaster she had faced in her marriage. But she had forgotten about that. It was the past and was over. She had pushed it into the deepest recesses of her mind. She had felt bitter and had been emotionally hurt when her marriage had gone down the rocks. But she had not allowed it to reflect on her life and had put it aside as one bad phase of her life. She didn't even recollect her past often. So how would it affect her now?

What was she thinking? She had to think of a way to treat Shivani, bring her back to normal and here she was thinking of herself. She was perfectly fine, happy with her career and moving on in life. She did not have any problems. Shivani had a problem and she as a psychiatrist was supposed to solve Shivani's problem.

Again her thoughts drifted back to what Swamiji had said. What had Swamiji said? He had spoken about peace and she longed to feel peaceful. She had always wanted to live peacefully and be content. She couldn't be content because as a woman she felt incomplete. She hadn't borne a child. But she had hardly been married for long. She didn't want to think of all that now. Her focus had to be on Shivani, the treatment and the solution.

All night she couldn't sleep. Peace, peace, peace – the words reverberated in the room. She would have to find peace and for that she would have to visit Swamiji's ashram. What was she thinking? Was she out of her mind? Swamiji was peaceful because he had done penance in the mountains. How could he give her peace? It was not a commodity. It was a feeling.

Why was this feeling of going and visiting Swamiji at his Ashram creeping in her mind again and again? Was she curious to know how he distributed peace? She giggled at her thought. She was going totally out of her mind. But one thing was very clear. Shivani had to become normal again. And she would have to think of a way to do that. Swamiji had told her to believe what Shivani had revealed. Amar's soul had been around, talking to Shivani and supporting her all the time. How was she going to tell this to Ragini or in fact anyone? They would all feel it was a ghost or something.

Swamiji's smile and his calm face seemed to be calling her to the ashram. Perhaps she should go there, see how the ashram was and how Swamiji treated people who had lost faith in the medical faculty. Yes, she would go there and see with her own eyes. Also the words 'peace' and 'journey homewards' were troubling her. She would go and ask Swamiji exactly what he had meant by that. She would go to the ashram. She made up her mind. With this thought in her mind, she slept off in the early hours of the morning.

Chapter 23

She woke up around eight in the morning. She was not feeling as tired or drained as she had expected she would. In fact, she was feeling more positive. The last thought before sleeping off and the first thought on waking up had been 'visit the ashram'.

She kept the saucepan to make some tea. She chuckled. A Swamiji had hypnotised a psychiatrist, into coming to visit his ashram. Hypnotised her! The thought made her laugh. It had been a long time since she had laughed. She felt lighter.

She stared out of the window sipping the tea slowly. The branches swayed and the dried leaves fell on the ground. She looked outside not seeing anything in particular. She would go and visit Swamiji at the ashram. She had nothing to lose. Also she was curious how she would get peace and the answer to all her questions from the ashram. She kept the cup on the table.

She called the travel agent to check if a ticket to Mangalore was available for tomorrow. Today she would speak to the Dean and ask for leave. She decided not to tell him about the ashram visit. It was not necessary. She would just take leave for a week stating 'family reasons' and later on extend if required. She hadn't availed of her paid leave in the last so many years since she had joined the Carewell hospital. She would tell Ragini that she was going to Mangalore for some research work and would return in a few days time. She knew Ragini would take good care of Shivani and anyway, in an emergency, she could always take her to the hospital. Sister Maya was visiting Shivani on a daily basis as an additional duty and Ragini had agreed to pay the nurse.

She decided against calling the ashram and informing them of her visit. She would just walk in and see. Some strong force was pulling her towards the ashram. The feeling was similar to the connection she felt for Shivani. She recalled her mom telling her many times to visit Mangalore. But she had been born in America and she had loved the place. India had never attracted her. Now this ashram was in Mangalore and she was going there. If her mom had been alive, she would have been so happy. Her demise had finally made Amartya quit America and come to India.

She sat in the plane again, third time in the same week. She was surprised that she who hated flying so much was so keen on taking a flight to Mangalore. Her mom's birth place was Mangalore and she had stayed there till her marriage after which she had permanently settled in the U.S. with her dad. Memories of her mom brought tears in her eyes and she stared out of the small window. India was beautiful, just like she had told her. She wished she had listened to her mom and come to India with her. Instead she had been adamant and had stayed back in the U.S.

Mangalore airport was not very big. She came out and saw many private taxis lined outside with the drivers ready to get hold of a passenger. A couple of them approached her asking "Where to madam?" She opened her purse to look at the address of the ashram which one of Swamiji's disciples had given her at the seminar. She took the paper to the first cab and asked the driver if he would take her to the ashram.

He looked at her as if he was more than a little surprised. Amartya wondered what was exactly wrong with her and why the driver was perusing her like a specimen.

After she settled in the cab, the driver asked her if she knew Swamiji. She told him that she had met Swamiji at a seminar and had been invited to the ashram.

"You are very lucky, madam. Not all people get an invitation to stay at the ashram. We see it from outside and hope that we too get an entry inside. But we do get to listen to Swamiji's *satsang* (discourses), you know lectures on God and spiritual stuff when he makes an appearance at the temple functions. He is a great man," he said. "And very powerful too," he added.

Amartya realized that her Anglo-Indian appearance had probably shocked the driver. She looked at herself in the rear-view mirror. Though her features were Indian, her skin colour and basic body structure was typically American. She was too fair and though after staying in India her skin had tanned, she still looked like an American.

"Madam, we have reached. I cannot take the cab inside. You have to walk through this small lane. It goes straight to the ashram entrance."

Amartya looked outside and saw a narrow pathway with trees on both sides. No vehicle could pass through the narrow road. She would have to walk. She stepped out of the cab.

"Thanks. I will walk down. How much do I pay you?"

"Madam, we normally charge double for foreigners or people who are new to the place. But somehow today I don't feel like doing that. Please give me Rs. 1000, the standard rate that we charge the locals."

Amartya smiled at the driver's explanation and gave him the fare and added another Rs.200 as tip.

He lifted her suitcase and kept it outside, gave her a salute and got inside the cab.

"I wish that your mission is successful, madam," the cab driver said and drove away in full speed.

Amartya stared at the taxi as it left a smoke of dust. When the smoke cleared she could see the pathway clearly. She stood rooted to the spot wondering what on earth she was doing in Mangalore. A five minute walk would lead her to the ashram. Why was she here?

She lifted the suitcase and started walking through the narrow pathway. It was a very peaceful place. She could hear the sound of birds chirping and the swish of the trees as they swayed with the breeze. She couldn't pull her suitcase along as there was only mud everywhere and no tarred road. The reddish brown mud crumbled through the high heels of her shoes. The heel sunk into the mud each time she took a step. But all this did not bother her. Something was pulling her towards the entrance which was visible now. She could see a huge iron gate. She reached the gate and looked around wondering whether to enter or wait for someone to come and open the gate. She saw a sentry running towards the gate.

"Yes madam?

That is all he said. Amartya wondered what to tell him.

"I am Dr. Amartya John. I want to meet Swamiji. I had met him at the seminar in Chennai and he had invited me to the Ashram. I do not know if he will remember but he had told me to come and see him at the ashram," she said.

The sentry entered the cabin near the gate and spoke on the intercom system to someone. He came out and said, "Yes madam, please come in."

He opened the gate and led her in. There was a huge garden on the right hand side. Beautiful pink and yellow flowers lined the garden on both sides. The grass had been trimmed to perfection. There was greenery all around the ashram building. She walked slowly absorbing the beauty of the place. As they walked past the garden, she saw a small one storey building. It looked very old.

"Madam, please go in. The third room to the right is Swamiji's room. He will see you now."

He walked away. Amartya climbed the steps and entered the main door which was open. She entered into a huge hall. It was like an auditorium. There was a small podium on the other end. Maybe this was where Swamiji sat while giving discourses. She knocked on the third door to her right and when she heard "please come in my child", she slowly opened the door.

She saw Swamiji sitting down on a mat on the floor. He looked divine. She left her suitcase at the door, removed her shoes and went inside. She stood in front of him.

"Sit down my child. So you decided to come."

So he remembered her. "Yes Swamiji, I truly want to help Shivani. I don't know why I have become so attached to her case. But I feel like I am the only person who can bring her back to normal and as I could not find any solution elsewhere, I came here."

She paused for a second and then continued, "Frankly speaking, Swamiji I really don't know what led me here. I am neither a religious nor a spiritual person. In fact, I hardly pray to God. I believe in science, I believe in research."

Amartya wondered what had gotten inside her and why she was saying all this in front of this reverend figure. She was speaking like a small kid. She looked up at Swamiji to check if he was angry. She was surprised to see a smile on his face.

"See child, you have come here not knowing exactly why you have come, right? It is okay. The divine energy and forces have pulled you here because this is the path you need to take. Do not question your own fate. You are flowing in the right direction. Nothing can go wrong from here."

Amartya sat silently feeling very pulled towards Swamiji's words. Somewhere deep inside her subconscious mind, she knew that she wanted peace and no science in this world was going to give it to her. But she had come to see if Swamiji could give her peace. If so, then how? But then again her mind did not want to accept anything that was not logical or scientific. And yet she was here. Was this destiny?

"Amartya, child, do not try to seek all the answers at once. You stay here at the ashram for a while. My pupils will tell you everything about the ashram and its rules. You can stay as long as you want. I am sure you will soon get your answers."

Amartya was shocked that Swamiji could read her mind so well. But then he was a powerful man with great sixth sense. She got up and stepped outside the room.

She saw two boys somewhere in their mid twenties wearing white kurta and dhoti standing outside. They looked pretty peaceful too, she observed. They had applied sandalwood paste on their forehead. When they saw her, they nodded and smiled at her and went inside Swamiji's room.

Amartya wondered if they were the ones who were going to help her settle in. Within a minute, they came out of Swamiji's room and introduced themselves.

"Dr. Amartya, I am Sivan and he is Raghu. Please give me your bag and we will guide you to your room."

"It is okay Sivan. I will carry the bag," said Amartya.

Amartya followed the boys as they guided her through the stairs leading to the first floor. There they opened the second door to the right. Everything was wooden. The doors, the staircase railing, the pillars were all made of wood. There were some carvings on the doors and pillars. She decided to check it out later.

Sivan said, "There are no specific rules for new comers to the ashram. This is your room. Every morning we, the pupils, other guest inmates like you residing in the ashram and Swamiji get up at 3 a.m. in the morning and take a dip in the pond which is there in the campus, just behind this building. We chant the holy mantras, and meditate for two hours. After this Swamiji retires to his room for *dhyaana* (meditation) and we go about doing the chores in the ashram. We take care of all the things needed by Swamiji and serve him. There is a kitchen and a pantry in the campus. It is outside this building. There is another small building just adjacent to this. You can see it from the window here.

Sivan pulled the curtains and she could see a small building.

He continued, "There are fixed timings for meals. The timings for each meal are written on a board outside the kitchen. The food prepared here is purely *satvic*, so it is low in spices and fat and is purely vegetarian."

Raghu said, "Madam, we do not know why you are here. But if Swamiji has invited you and you have come, it means that you are seeking some answers. Every person who has ever come to the ashram and been under Swamiji's grace has always received all the answers. Just follow his words. His words hold a lot of meaning. He will slowly guide you and teach you how to meditate and understand your deeper self. Please feel comfortable and ask us for anything that you need. We are always somewhere around this building which we call the main ashram building either doing chores, meditating with Swamiji or listening to his discourses which we call *satsang*."

Amartya looked at the boys who were so young and yet so spiritual. They looked peaceful and had a bit of the divinity that she had seen in Swamiji. Why had they devoted their life to the ashram and not living a merry life outside? They were so young…

After the boys left, Amartya sat down on the single bed placed in the corner of the room. The room was small but comfortable. There was a small cupboard to keep clothes. It was made of teak wood. There was a bathroom which was modern and very clean. There was one window with white curtains.

She looked out of the window. She saw a ground floor structure, which was the kitchen. She could see a pond on the left side. It was surrounded by trees on three sides. The ground was clean and there were trees all around. Occasionally, she heard the sound of birds chirping. There was no sound other than that. She wondered how many people stayed in the ashram. She sat down on the bed thinking about destiny. What had brought her to this place? It was so quiet and peaceful here. She dozed off.

Chapter 24

When she woke up the room was dark. She saw light filtering in through the windows. It was a full moon night. She was so used to sleeping in the comfort of the air conditioner; she was surprised that she had slept off without even switching on the fan in the room. She looked on the wall to check the time. There was no clock. She checked the time on her wrist watch. It was 7 p.m. She wondered if all the inmates of the ashram had already called it a day. If everyone got up at 3 a.m., surely they might have slept off by now.

She looked out of the window to see if there was light in the kitchen building. The kitchen was well lit. Her stomach was growling with hunger. She freshened up and closed the door of her room. There was no lock. Obviously, there wouldn't be any theft taking place in an ashram. She had been conditioned over the years to lock up carefully while leaving the house. She smiled at the thought. She climbed down the stairs and saw Sivan who was walking out of the building. She called him and he stood there waiting for her to reach him.

"Sivan, I am hungry and I hoped I would get something to eat in the kitchen."

"Sure doctor. The evening meal timings are 7 p.m. to 8.30 p.m. Please go and have your dinner. Some pupils are still having dinner and some guests like you are also there."

Amartya walked towards the kitchen. She inhaled the aroma of home cooked food floating in the air.

She hadn't eaten in the plane and after reaching the ashram she had slept off. She had not even had coffee. Now she could hear her stomach growling. She walked faster. She entered into a huge hall. There were many tables and chairs arranged neatly in a row. There were floor mats for people who preferred to sit on the floor and eat.

Across the room she saw a large table with a delightful spread of various food items. She picked up a plate, aware that there were many others in the hall eating food, but still concentrating only on the food kept on the table. The food seemed all new to her. She had grown up eating meat and fish and even in Kolkata she ate more of fish and rice. There were two curries, one red and the other yellow. In the next container, she guessed it was green peas and potatoes and in another she saw cabbage mixed with grated coconut. Then there was finely chopped cucumber and carrot mixed in curd and a green salad made of mixed sprouts and pomegranate seeds garnished with coriander leaves. It all looked absolutely colourful and divine.

She took some rice on her plate and poured a ladle full of both curries in small round steel bowls. She lingered over the vegetables and finally just took a large spoonful of the vegetables and the mixed sprouts salad. She hoped it would taste as delicious as it looked. After filling up her plate, she finally turned and looked around her. She could easily identify the disciples as they wore either white or saffron clothes. Then there were some guests like her. They were wearing coloured clothes but had a saffron shawl around their necks. She did not feel like talking to anyone. She sat down at a table a little away from the others and slowly started eating the food.

The food was very tasty. Nothing was spicy, just the way she liked it. There were no strong tastes of garlic or onion. The food tasted mild and was very soothing on the stomach. They should serve such food to patients in their Hospital in Kolkata, she thought.

She relished the food and was surprised that she had eaten all that she had taken on her plate. She observed that all of them were washing their plates at the sink outside. She picked up her plate and walked towards the sink. She saw a lady who was wearing a white sari walking out of the kitchen. The lady smiled at her.

Amartya smiled back and saw that the lady was quite old maybe in her sixties.

"Did you enjoy your meal?" the woman asked.

"Yes, it was delicious. I would like to thank the person who prepared it," replied Amartya.

"All the disciples and inmates of the ashram do the chores at the ashram. We divide it amongst ourselves. This week two other ladies and I are in charge of cooking and cleaning the kitchen. You can join us too! We take turns to keep the ashram clean and equipped. Even Swamiji does so much work here. He takes care of the cows and the plants. We all live like a family here."

She walked towards the main building. So there were many pupils and other inmates here and all of them took care of the ashram by doing some chore. Amartya was happy that everyone was treated equally at the ashram.

Amartya's mom used to stay in Mangalore. Had she ever met Swamiji? She had left Mangalore many years ago when she had been just 22 years old. She had met her dad and fallen in love with him and gone away to the U.S. Maybe she had not seen Swamiji at all. But this ashram looked very old. Almost a hundred years old. Maybe her mom had visited the ashram and met some other Swamiji at that time. Probably that was what had drawn her here.

She climbed the stairs and walked towards her room. Would she see Swamiji tomorrow? She had only a week's leave and so many questions were still unanswered. She was doubtful if she would be able to sleep after the long siesta in the evening. Normally, she would have felt eerie at the thought of staying in a small room with dim lights and no sound, no television, no internet connection. But instead she enjoyed the silence. She decided to lie down on the bed and actually think out her thoughts clearly. But she slept off.

Chapter 25

It was somewhere in the wee hours of the morning that Amartya woke up. She could hear chants. The sound of chanting was not loud but there was a vibration. She checked her watch. It was 4 a.m. She wanted to sleep until morning and so she pulled the sheets over her head. But she couldn't sleep. She got up and went to the bathroom. She took a quick wash, dressed up and went down. She entered the main hall and saw it was filled with people. All of them were sitting on the floor on individual mats. They were all chanting some words with their eyes closed. The unification with which they were chanting was amazing.

Amartya saw a woman wearing a white sari enter the hall. The woman motioned her to come. Was she the same woman who had spoken to her yesterday night after dinner in the kitchen? They all looked the same to her. Amartya walked towards the woman and realized it was not the same lady. This lady was younger; somewhere in her forties and had beautiful long hair which she had tied in two plaits. She gave her a mat, sat down and joined the others in the chanting. Amartya looked around, saw everyone busy chanting and decided to sit down and join everyone. She sat on the mat and closed her eyes. She could not get the exact words of the chant but she started feeling a strange vibration after closing her eyes. The words reverberated in the hall and Amartya started feeling peaceful.

After a while, the sound stopped and Amartya opened her eyes. She saw Swamiji seated on the dais with his eyes closed. All the others had opened their eyes and were waiting with bated breath for Swamiji to open his eyes and speak.

Amartya looked around and saw many men and women of all ages sitting quietly with their hands folded. Did they all stay here?

There were around twenty people in the room. The building had around fifteen to twenty rooms. So yes, it was quite possible for so many people to stay here. But though twenty people stayed under one roof, hardly any sound was heard. And suddenly there was a hushed silence and she saw that Swamiji had opened his eyes. He looked so divine.

"Bless you all my dear children. Today I will speak about the mantras that we chant. Why do we chant mantras? What are these words, at times a combination of words that we call a mantra? These mantras originate from ancient scriptures and are very powerful. When we chant the mantras, they create an energy vibration which merges with the universal energy. Who do you think you are? We are all just energy. And when we chant these divine mantras, we combine our energy with the universal energy and the vibrations created are very powerful."

Amartya was lost in Swamiji's words. Most of this she knew. Of course she knew about atoms, cells and molecules and that living beings were just energy and all that. Swamiji was telling everything she knew. But still the way he was saying it, made more sense. It was less scientific and more spiritual the way Swamiji presented the whole thing.

She wanted to know more about the mantras. She had never heard the mantras and she liked listening to them. She decided to meet Swamiji and ask him to teach her the mantras. She too would chant and experience the vibration that she had felt in the hall a while ago.

Swamiji spoke for about two hours and then the people in the room bowed their hands in reverence and started leaving one by one. Amartya did not get up and waited till most of them had left. Then she got up and went near Swamiji.

"Amartya, how are you feeling today?" he asked.

"I am fine Swamiji. Actually I wanted to talk to you yesterday but I just slept off. Today I was awakened by the chanting and came down. I am surprised I slept so much. I generally don't sleep this much."

Amartya wondered why she was saying so much about her sleep and not coming to the point. But Swamiji seemed to have guessed what was going on in her mind. He said, "When you came here you had some issues to resolve. You were very tensed and worried. But as soon as you entered the ashram, the peace and tranquillity of the place attracted you. You felt relaxed and slept blissfully. There is a lot of positive energy in this place. You will soon absorb the energy and start feeling more positive. Your thoughts will be clearer and soon you will have your answers."

"Swamiji, I want to learn the mantras. I felt a vibration today when I entered the hall. I want to feel it within myself by chanting the mantras. But I do not know the words. Could you please teach me?" she asked.

Swamiji nodded and closed his eyes. After a while, he opened his eyes and blessed her. He whispered a special mantra in her ear. He then wrote it on a piece of paper and gave it to her. He also gave her a book which had some of the mantras that she had heard a while ago. He told her that the special mantra he had given her was for her alone to chant in her free time.

He reminded her that though she was a guest, she would have to help out in the ashram. Amartya recalled what Swamiji had said, "Never take anything for free and never give anything for free."

It was so true. She went out to the kitchen building and decided to join the others in cooking. She found that all the people were very friendly and no one had any airs. Each one of them was just trying to do his or her best in whatever chore they were doing. No one was big or small. There was no status issue.

She enjoyed her morning in the kitchen and then decided to water the plants in the evening. She went up to her room to learn the mantras. She started reciting the mantras and was soon very engrossed. Each alphabet had a separate vibration and she could actually feel it. She learnt the special mantra that Swamiji had given her. After a while, she closed her eyes and started chanting it.

When she opened her eyes, she felt energised and strong as though she had eaten some magic potion of vitamins or something.

All of a sudden she realized that she had come here to seek some answers for Shivani. She had totally forgotten about it. The mantra and chants etc. had taken her mind away from her main mission. Was she getting trapped in some kind of a fraudulent process? She had heard of many fake swamis who were big cheats and cheated people of their money and all. But this Swamiji had not asked anything from her. He had just given her some mantra to chant and that too on her request. She was a psychiatrist! What was she afraid of? As if someone could hypnotise her or fool her! What was she thinking?

In the evening she would go and meet Swamiji and directly ask him for the answers. She wanted to know how Amar could speak to Shivani or how Shivani could meet Amar long after he was dead. She wanted to know the mystery of the soul. She did know souls existed but obviously they were always in some physical body. How could Amar have the same physical body after he had died and his body had been cremated?

She knew for sure that there were no spirits and ghosts and never believed in all that crap. She would speak to Swamiji and if he did not have the answers she would leave tomorrow. She had to go back to her life and career and she had no intention of wasting time here.

In the evening, Swamiji gave a discourse again. This time some outsiders had been allowed and the hall was totally packed with people.

He began, "Who are you? Are you the physical body or are you the soul? Why have you taken birth? What is the purpose of your birth? Each one of you in this hall has to think about this. I know one will say he is a doctor, the other an engineer or a housewife or something. But is that what you are? 'A somebody' is that all you are? If not, then why are you here? Why are you always afraid of death? Who dies? The soul? Or the body? Tell me, does anyone know who dies? If you think that the soul is attached to the body and when the body dies, the soul dies, then, my dear children you are all so wrong. The soul is immortal. We have all heard this and read this but actually do not believe in this. The soul never dies. Now I know you will ask what happens to the soul when a person dies and his body is buried or cremated. The soul enters another body. Many of you might know this."

"So why are we so attached to this physical body? Why do we take so much care of our body, our hands, legs etc? We are so particular that not a single mark should appear on the body. Yet, the physical body is most of the time undergoing some suffering. You will say my hands are paining, legs are paining, and head is aching and so on. Then one day the body dies. It is over. That is what you think. The person is gone. Dead, finished, never to return... But the soul is there seeing us when we cry over the body. The soul feels bad and cries too. Don't cry. Chant the mantras, perform *pujas, homa* and listen to *satsang* and pray for the soul. Don't hold on to the soul. Let go."

"But we do not do that. We hold on to the soul, hoping that the body will become alive again knowing that it is not going to happen. Our mind is so possessive about the dead person that even after cremating the body we hope and dream that the person will come alive again. We cling on to the dead person. The soul never departs in such cases. The soul of the person stays with us. But the soul has a journey and till you hold on to the soul, its journey is incomplete. Let go! Let go of your attachment. Everyone who has taken birth will go one day. But remember it is the body that we shed and the soul lives on, but in another body. Do not create hindrance for the soul. Let the soul carry on its journey."

Swamiji ended his discourse.

Chapter 26

Amartya could hear people whispering. They were all discussing what Swamiji had said about the soul. The person sitting next to her said, "I have some doubts. I could ask Swamiji but it is not necessary. Next week when I come to listen to Swamiji, he will speak only about what I want to know. It is always like that. We just need to think of our problem or question and surprisingly Swamiji will speak only about that problem and the solution for that on that particular day."

Another said, "I believe in Swamiji. He has done a lot of *sadhana*. He has all the answers. Big big doctors become dumbfounded in front of Swamiji. He is a sea of knowledge. No one has left this place without clearing his doubt. He is like God to me. I feel very peaceful after listening to Swamiji's discourses. Now after this break, there will be *bhajans* and *kirtans*. We will all be singing some songs in praise of the Almighty God. Some of them will be playing the instruments. I feel at peace after the *bhajans*."

Amartya listened to them without commenting. She did not know what would happen during the *bhajans*. She got up and sat at the extreme end of the hall. She hoped she would be able to speak to Swamiji after that. The *bhajans* were very touching and she felt like singing along with the others but did not know the words of the songs. She clapped along with the others and soon got immersed in the tunes.

The *bhajans* made her feel very peaceful. When everyone started dispersing, Amartya looked across at the dais hoping Swamiji hadn't left. But he was sitting there talking to some people. When they left, Amartya walked up to Swamiji.

"Yes child, you ask what you want to ask."

Amartya was surprised that Swamiji had read her mind. Was he a mind reader too?

"Swamiji, I had told you about Shivani and that she had been seeing her dead father. At least that is what she mumbled when she saw the photograph of her father on my desk. I am unable to understand how this is possible. I wanted to know much in depth about souls and their entity."

"I will answer your question, Amartya. But you will still not believe me. You will seek proof which I don't have. Shivani's father died but his soul never left. He probably felt he had some half done tasks and lingered on. And Shivani was very attached to her father and so started seeing his soul. Obviously, she couldn't see the soul as it is just energy. She visualised the body of her father and the soul spoke to her. Again no words need to be uttered. The communication is between two energy bodies. Souls can communicate with each other. Words are just a physical form of speech. He was never present in the actual physical form like you are imagining."

"But Swamiji, she had mentioned in her diary that she did not recollect the face of her parents."

"Shivani might not have known how her father looked like. But her subconscious mind might have stored an image of her father who she loved the most. And when she heard the soul speak to her, she visualised the same face. Her conscious mind never realized that it was her father's image and so she never wrote it in her diary."

Amartya sat silently for a moment trying to absorb what Swamiji had said. Somehow she could not make herself believe all this.

"I knew that after being educated in the field of psychiatry, you will find all this very illogical and unbelievable. But child, there is no other explanation to this. For you to actually trust what I am saying, you need to do *sadhana* and chant the mantra that I have given you. You should join us for mediation at 3 a.m. in the morning. We all sit down and meditate for one hour or more and then start chanting the mantras. The energy level in group meditation is very high and the early morning hour is the time when the universal consciousness is at its peak. It is very easy to merge our energy with the universal energy at that time. All this will invoke the inner you and make you see the truth. My words will not be sufficient for you to believe the facts. When you listen to someone say something or you read something, it is always a belief. But once you experience it, it becomes the ultimate truth."

Swamiji continued, "You are trapped in some deep misery. I can see it. But you can't. You feel you are a successful doctor, well settled and going in the right direction. But somewhere deep inside, you are seeking some answers for yourself. There is some insecurity within you which pulls you towards Shivani who is also in the same boat. You feel a strange connection to Shivani, don't you?"

Amartya marvelled at how Swamiji knew so much that went on within her mind without actually hypnotising her. How could he sense her insecurities? But what he said was true. She had been wondering why Shivani's case had attracted her so much. Why had she felt so responsible for Shivani? Probably, they both shared the same insecurities.

Shivani's father had died when she was a small girl and her mother had left her and gone away with some other man. In her case, her dad had gone away with another woman. She still remembered how much her mom had cried. She had been unable to bear the sorrow. She had cried for weeks on end.

"Don't cry child. You have to let go of these emotions," consoled Swamiji.

Amartya touched her cheeks which were wet with tears. She had not even realized that she was crying.

"The solution for this is to stay here for some time. I will teach you several types of *sadhana*, meditation and chants. You will get your answers. You won't need my help after that. It is not about

Shivani alone. It is also about you, Amartya. You need to resolve the issues that are stored deep inside your mind. You need to let go of the hurt and bitterness that you have stored. It is only after you have evolved that, you can tackle cases of mental instability in other persons and be a successful doctor."

Swamiji kept his hand over her head and blessed her.

Amartya got up and walked slowly to her room. What had Swamiji said? Did she have bitterness and hurt stored inside her? Yes, she did have some unresolved issues stored in the deepest corner of her mind. But they were all over. At least that is what she thought.

She had left everything behind and come to India, hadn't she? Had she not left all the hurt and tears back in the U.S.?

She had travelled thousands of kilometres to get away from the place where she had seen distrust and pain. But had she actually left behind the sentiments or brought it along with her to India? Had she been fooling herself?

Amartya was feeling very restless and she felt like running away – back to Kolkata to the hospital where she could treat patients and live her routine life. She was earning well, was happy and had a good social status. She was secure there. *Or wasn't she?*

Was running away the answer? She had run away from the U.S. to India but still hadn't left the pain behind. And now she was thinking of running away from the ashram back to her secure cocoon in Kolkata. Was she secure? Or was she making a web of security and trying to feel secure in it?

How long would she run and how far? She would have to stop at some time and sit back and think. Her life was simply a routine where she thought she was happy. But deep inside she knew she was not happy. She had wanted more from life and the fact that she had been unable to get all that had disappointed her so much that she had suppressed her emotions and made a facade of false emotions which gave her false security.

Where was she going? Did her life have any meaning? Of course, it had. She was treating so many people and was quite successful in her field. She had put in so much effort in the initial years after her degree. She had worked with several doctors and had gained very good experience. That was how she had been able to easily get the designation of an independent resident psychiatrist at the Carewell Hospital in India. The struggle had paid off. She had been self-sufficient and satisfied till she had taken up Shivani's case.

Shivani's case made her feel that her knowledge was incomplete. But most of the experienced doctors hadn't been able to help her. She had come here to seek answers from Swamiji. How was it possible that highly experienced psychiatrists hadn't been able to give her the answers? They all had said that hypnotism and shock therapy was the solution. Why then had she not taken their advice and gone ahead. Why was she feeling so much emotion for Shivani? Amartya went on thinking late into the night.

Chapter 27

She awakened early in the morning at 3 a.m. She took bath, draped her light blue and white sari and went to the hall downstairs. She took a mat and joined the others who were meditating. There was absolute silence in the hall. She sat down cross-legged on the mat and closed her eyes. Her thoughts continued from where she had left off the previous night.

She had slept off thinking of Shivani. She wondered what she was doing at the ashram meditating instead of taking care of her patients back in Kolkata. Her thoughts drifted. The silence around her was disturbing. She felt very conscious of the silence. There were at least fifteen people in the hall meditating in silence. What were these people thinking? How were they meditating? Did meditation mean silence? Were they not having an inner conversation with themselves? She found it impossible to not think or just be silent. Even though she was not uttering a single word, her mind was racing with innumerable thoughts. Her thoughts slowly drifted to her past.

She had come home from school and her mom had been crying. She had never seen her cry before that. She had explained to her that her dad had left them. She had been just eight years old. She had felt so shocked. How would they go on living without him? Why had he left them? So many questions and she had no answers. But her mom had been strong, at least externally. She had been working and she continued with her job. They moved into a smaller apartment and with the alimony and her salary, she had managed to raise her well. And when Amartya had been in her teens, she had realized that her dad had gone away with an American woman. She had asked her mom why he had left them.

Amartya's mom had explained that she was an Indian and he had got bored with her and married one of his own types. She remembered the hurt in her voice. She had vowed not to get involved with any boy and had concentrated on her studies. Psychiatry had interested her since childhood and she had wanted to understand and explore the inner depths of the human mind. Why had her dad left them? What emotion had he missed from her mom that had pulled him to another woman of his own community? Mom had left India after falling in love with dad and had severed all ties with her family and relatives. And ten years after the marriage, he had left her.

She remembered telling her mom to call all her relatives in India and get in touch with them but she had refused. After Amartya had completed her degree and had started her career as a psychiatrist, her mom had wanted them to go to India. But Amartya did not feel like going to a country of people who had so easily severed ties with a daughter who had gone away with an American. So what if she had left her parents to go away with an American man? Why hadn't they tried to trace her mom or stay in touch? Every third day her mom would ask her if they could go back to Mangalore. That is where she belonged. But Amartya had adamantly refused to go to India. Her mom had silently accepted her decision.

Amartya was jolted back to the present when she heard the loud chant of 'OM'.

She instinctively joined the others. The entire room was filled with instant energy. The sound of 'OM' was reverberating in circles. The room was filled with the echo of 'OM'. She started chanting the mantras along with the others.

It was a beautiful experience. She felt so much peace. How could a few words create such an effect? What was this chant and why was there so much vibration in it? She knew Swamiji would clear her doubts.

Amartya felt like speaking to Swamiji. After the morning session was over, she walked up to him. She wanted to convey how peaceful she was feeling.

"You are feeling good, aren't you?"

How had Swamiji known what she was feeling? And as if on cue Swamiji said, "Your eyes reflect deep peace".

"Yes Swamiji, I am feeling very peaceful. I wonder what the mantras mean. How could some words create so much vibration? What is this? I want to know scientifically how you would explain this feeling of peace."

Swamiji looked at her and she saw so much peace and tranquillity in his eyes. His voice had a vibration and when he spoke, she felt even more peaceful.

"This is all energy. The universe around you is made up of energy. When you chant certain words, they create some energy and vibrate. The universal energy connects to it. So you feel a vibration. These chants are from the ancient scriptures and are very effective. There is a mantra for everything. You will always get what you seek. So child, what are you actually seeking? What is it that you want?"

"I want a method to cure Shivani and explain to her that she wasn't seeing Amar."

"Is that why you travelled till here? Ask your inner self. There is a different purpose. I can see it. But I cannot tell you. It is for you to find out. Ask yourself when you meditate. What is your purpose of coming all the way till here?"

Amartya nodded, bowed and took Swamiji's blessings. She went about her chores. She had taken up the task of gardening and helping in the kitchen. She actually enjoyed doing the work. Life was different at the ashram and though people didn't speak as much or converse with each other a lot, she never felt lonely. Not the way she used to feel at the hospital with so many people around her. The energy around her was so positive that she felt radiant and alive.

Amartya fixed the alarm on her watch. She wanted to be on time for the meditation. Living at the ashram was making her realize how simple life actually was.

Next morning when she reached the meditation hall, it was half empty. She had reached early and many people were yet to join for the meditation. Within five minutes, she saw that the entire hall was full. Nobody spoke to anyone. Each one took a mat and sat down and closed their eyes. Amartya followed suit.

She saw Swamiji. He looked so peaceful even with his eyes closed. Why was she always observing that one thing? Was she missing peace so much? Did that mean she was not peaceful? She had felt peaceful while chanting. But later on her mind had been in turmoil again. She closed her eyes.

Amartya's mom was basically from Mangalore and had been born, brought up and educated in Mangalore. She wished she knew where her grandparents were if at all they were alive. She wanted to see the place where her mom had lived... Her thoughts drifted to her past again.

After she had joined the hospital, her mom had wanted to go to India. But she had never felt the desire to see India. She had been busy with her work. She rarely had time to speak to her mom. But her mom had always understood and supported her.

She gained very good experience in her field and soon she started seeing patients independently. Many of her patients preferred to seek her advice and liked her method of counselling. She had planned to open her own clinic. That is when she had met Gary John at the cafe…

She had completed the last shift at the hospital and had been extremely tired. She had not wanted to have coffee at the hospital mess and so had opted to have coffee at the cafe across the street. It had been winter, very cold and the cafe had been absolutely full. She hadn't found a seat and she had turned to walk out when she had seen a man sitting in the corner. He was alone and the seat opposite him had been vacant. She had walked up to him and he had confirmed that he was alone. He had struck up a great conversation and though initially, she had not wanted to talk to him, she had enjoyed his company. Later on she had been surprised that she had spoken to an absolute stranger and even enjoyed his company.

She had vowed never to get involved with men except professionally. She had felt an aversion for men after her dad had left them and yet she had talked to Gary John for more than half an hour.

After she had walked out of the cafe she had admonished herself for having fallen for his good looks. She had vowed never to make the mistake again. But eventually she had gone to the cafe the next day just to check if Gary was there. And he was sitting at the same place as though waiting for her. Gary was not very tall. He was stout, fair, had a moustache, light brown hair and looked extremely good. He always rubbed his stubble while thinking. She had found him to be a very charming gentleman. After several meetings she had fallen in love. He had confessed quite early in their relationship that he had found her very attractive right from the first day he had seen her. After six months he had proposed marriage.

She had spoken to her mom and had been shocked at the way she had reacted. She still remembered her words,"Have you gone out of your mind? I, an Indian ran away from India with your dad and very conveniently he left me for an American woman. You were so young at that time. But he didn't care. He was lovesick and had forgotten that he had a wife and child at home. This man you are planning to marry is also an American. And don't forget Amartya that you are half Indian. You might be going around with the name 'Amartya Smith' but don't forget you have my genes too. Harry cheated me and left me. I don't want you facing the same thing. I have taken one shock in my life. I cannot take another."

And then she had melted and cried. "Amartya, please do not marry Gary. He will eventually get tired of you and leave you. What will you do then? Suppose you have a child from your marriage, do you know how difficult it is to bring up a child without a husband to support you? I have suffered a lot of insecurity and stress after Harry left me. I love you too much to see you undergo anything that I went through."

Amartya recalled convincing her that Gary was not like her dad and he wouldn't leave her. She had cried so much. She had just mumbled that her heart would break if ever her fears turned true.

Amartya had felt at that time that her mom had simply created a lot of negative emotions and was unnecessarily thinking that her daughter would face the same thing that she had faced.

Amartya had married Gary John after two months. Her mom had been very unhappy with her decision.

The chants brought her back to the present. She started chanting with the others. She started feeling relaxed. The thoughts of her past had made her tense and stiff. And as she started chanting, she started feeling more relaxed and peaceful.

When she went up to her room for her afternoon siesta, she realized that whatever Swamiji had said was correct. She had been very restless. Though she had felt that she had come for solving Shivani's case, she had actually come out of curiosity. She had wanted to know why Swamiji had said that if she wanted peace, she could come to the ashram. She had been attracted by the word 'peace' and how conveniently she had fooled her conscious mind that she had come to seek answers for Shivani.

Yes, she had come to seek answers, but it had not been for Shivani. It had been for herself. Somewhere in her subconscious mind she knew she had many questions and unresolved issues. Her past had been tormenting her and still was...

Her marriage to Gary John had been dreamlike for the first one year. She had enjoyed so much that she had hoped her mom would also smile and be happy. But she had never been happy. She had always felt that Gary would leave her daughter who would be then left alone. How right she had been!

After the first year, her responsibilities at the hospital had increased and many a times she would have to work night shifts. Gary had initially not minded but after a while he had started complaining. He did not understand her work pressures at all. He was working with a software company and used to get home by 6 p.m. in the evening. He had hated waiting for her at nights and had started cribbing about it. She had started retorting as she couldn't take the pressure at the hospital and at home. She had expected her dear Gary would understand. But he hadn't. She had tried many a times to explain about her work and the pressures. She had promised him that in a year she could start her own clinic and then she would be able to keep flexible timings after that. But all that had fallen on deaf ears.

One evening when she had returned home early, she had seen a woman in Gary's arms. She had not even waited for an explanation and had walked out of her house straight to her mom's house.

Her mom had cried more than she had. Somehow she had taken Gary's affair in her stride. But her mom had been shocked, fallen sick and had been hospitalized. A month after the discharge, she had a fatal heart attack. Amartya had felt like her whole world had collapsed. She still remembered finishing all the formalities in the U.S. and applying for work in India. She had immediately decided to leave U.S.

Gary had come and apologized but she had not listened to his explanation. There was no explanation for an extra marital affair. It was clearly understood that he had lost interest in her. She never regretted her decision of divorce.

And she had flown to India as soon as she had received her appointment at the Carewell Hospital, Kolkata. Her dream to start her own clinic could wait.

Chapter 28

Amartya decided to send a mail asking for leave extension. It was a fortnight now since she had come to the ashram. She knew the Dean would be upset and angry that she was taking unwarranted leave. But somehow it did not matter now. She was very happy at the ashram and wanted to stay on till she received all the answers.

Nobody knew where she was and she did not think it necessary to inform anyone. She sent a message to the hospital that she would be on indefinite leave due to certain personal issues. The Dean would probably look for a replacement, she thought. She was not bothered. She knew that with her experience she would easily get placed as a resident psychiatrist at any hospital. That was not what was troubling her. It was her past that tormented her. It was like she had no control over her thoughts. The incidents just went on floating in front of her eyes. It was like a dam that had burst and now the water had to flow… without control…

Swamiji had said '*forgive everyone*' and she had been trying It was so difficult to forgive her dad and Gary. Both had destroyed her life. She remembered every word of what Swamiji had said yesterday at the discourse.

He had said, "Forgive everyone in your life. Every person who you feel has hurt you in some way. They did what they had come here to do. It is all karmic. They had come in your life to settle their karmic account with you. If some person has hurt you or is troubling you, it is because in some past life you must have done the same to that person. All our actions are governed by our karma. We are born with a karmic account."

"Unless the karmic debts are cleared, the soul cannot complete its journey. Karmic accounts are both good and bad. Many a times you wonder why some person who loves you a lot gives you immense happiness. We are all here for a purpose. Every person you encounter in your life has come to settle some account with you. There is no co-incidence. Each person has come in your life with a reason. Don't question. Just accept and settle the account without creating negative emotions. Because as soon as you create a negative emotion, you create another karmic account and the cycle continues. Every soul originally seeks self enlightenment but during the course of its journey forgets everything as *maya* grips the soul. *Maya* is the desires of the physical body."

"So you all have to realize that unless you learn to forgive all the people who have hurt you in this life or the previous lives, you cannot live peacefully. Just forgive and seek forgiveness. When you are meditating you must seek forgiveness from all the souls that you might have hurt. You need not recollect any particular incident or person. Just send forgiveness and the universe will accept it. The forgiveness will go to all the souls who knowingly or unknowingly have hurt you. They will thank you for releasing them. Similarly, seek forgiveness from all the souls who you might have hurt. You will be forgiven and released from your negative karma and your paths will clear."

Amartya did not know how to forgive her dad. He had left them alone and gone away with another woman. She did not feel like forgiving him. But it had been so many years ago. She would have to forgive him. But her mom had never forgiven him. She remembered once he had phoned her mom and how she had blasted at him saying, "Don't show me your face ever again. I hate you." She missed her mom.

Her dad was probably there somewhere in the U.S. He had never called or she had never seen him after he had left them and gone away. Maybe he had left the U.S, and gone somewhere else. But how did that matter. She had a big task of forgiving the man who had made her life insecure for no fault of hers. But Swamiji always said that what we faced in our life was our karma and blaming others for our sorrow would simply increase our negative karma. She would have to forgive her dad though he had broken her mom's heart. What had Swamiji said? *'We all are here to clear our karmic debts.'* Did that mean that she had been destined to be insecure and lonely? Whatever she had gone through all her life till now was all destined? Her marriage to Gary, the divorce had all been destined? If so, had destiny pulled her here to the ashram? Was she seeking self-realization?

But Swamiji had also said that people had the power to change their destiny provided they knew the right path. There was so much to learn and she was actually getting deeply involved in spirituality and enjoying the experience as well. She was feeling more complete as a person now.

She set her alarm for 2.45 a.m. She knew she no longer needed the alarm as she would awaken automatically around that time. Still the alarm which was just an external object seemed more dependable. She smiled. Every day she was getting up just before the alarm rang. Still smiling, she slept off.

She got up before the alarm rang and rushed to the meditation hall. There weren't many people today. She took a mat and sat down. She closed her eyes. She thought of her mom.

She started seeking forgiveness from her. She shouldn't have married Gary John. She should have listened to her. When Gary had left her just like her mom had predicted he would, she had been unable to take the shock. She had passed away.

Amartya felt she was the reason for her mom's death. She always blamed herself and wished she had listened to her and come to India after completing her education. But instead she had joined the hospital and then eventually met Gary. "Mom, I am so sorry for not listening to you. I am to blame for your demise. You would have been alive today had I listened to you."Amartya went on praying and seeking forgiveness and then she saw her.

She said, "How are you Amartya? I am glad that you have come to India. I have come to clear some of your doubts. I know you have been feeling guilty and blame yourself for my demise. Don't go on torturing yourself. My time had come and I had to leave. I had built up too much negative karma and so had to leave early. I felt like my life had no meaning and I could clear all my mistakes by taking another birth. I will soon go away and enter another body. My deepest wish had been to see you at peace with yourself. Now you are on the right path. Don't blame yourself for anything. Harry left me because he was not a stable person. But I blamed myself all my life. I felt like I was not good enough for him. I had left all my people behind in India and severed ties with them. I had nowhere to turn to. Also, I was very egoistic. I didn't want to turn to anyone later on. Harry had called me once. He had been keeping low health and his second wife was not taking care of him. He had asked me if he could come back. I had told him that I never wanted to see his face again. My insecurity had turned into false pride and anger. I never forgave him. But Amartya, you have to forgive your dad. What he did was wrong but he was not a bad person at heart. He did what his karma led him to do."

She continued, "You did not even listen to Gary's explanation and divorced him. He doesn't know where you are and has no means to contact you. You either forgive him or at least call him and speak to him. Don't leave any work half done in your life. Don't create karmic debts. Release everyone from your life. Don't remain tied to people by hurting or feeling hurt. I am really glad that you are here at the ashram with Swamiji. He will guide you in the right manner. When I was young I used to come with my mother to this ashram. At that time Guruji, who was Swamiji's guru used to give discourses. I will go now. Live a peaceful life from now on."

Amartya opened her eyes. She had felt like she had been having a loud conversation with her mom and everyone else would have been roused from their meditation. But no one had seen or heard anything. They were all sitting in deep meditation.

So it was true. Souls existed and they did communicate. Her face was damp with tears. She had cried. But now she was feeling happy and light. It was as if a huge burden had been lifted from her shoulders. She was free. Almost! She still had to forgive her dad and Gary. She would do that.

Everyone started the chants and she joined them. She was smiling. She felt exhilarated. When she was leaving, Swamiji called her.

"Child, are you relieved of some burden today?"

Amartya looked at Swamiji totally surprised. How had he known?

"No souls can enter this ashram without my knowledge. I am in constant connection with the universal energy. Why are you surprised? Aren't you an energy body? So why do you find it surprising that a soul can communicate with another soul. Aren't you a soul? Do you think you are a body? Souls communicate. Now your mother's soul is free to continue the journey. I am glad you have received most of your answers. Haven't you?"

"Yes Swamiji, I thank you for that. Something was pulling me here right from the time I saw you at the seminar. I gave hundreds of explanations for my coming here but never admitted that there was some universal pull, something, I couldn't place my hand on which was dragging me here. Swamiji, we all have an inner voice, don't we?"

"Yes child, we all have an inner voice. We are the soul and this body is just like a garment for us which we eventually shed when we have finished our chores for this life. We then take another form, another body and the journey continues. But the karmic account also continues. It does not finish with the body. It goes with the soul. So, we must listen to the inner voice because it is our own voice. The voice of the soul..."

Amartya walked out of the hall feeling peaceful. She had seen her mom. Mom had forgiven dad and now she too would forgive him. She did not want to meet him or call him up. But she would send forgiveness while meditating. She did not want to remain tied to him because of her negative emotions. She wanted to release him from her life. She wanted to release all her insecurities and fears, the hurt and the anger from her life. She wanted to feel completely free.

And she would have to call Gary and speak to him. She would listen to whatever he had to say. That is in case he wanted to speak to her. Either way it didn't matter now. If he felt like talking, she would talk and listen to his explanation or she would just forgive him. None of that was important now. Her mom had guided her in the right way today. But her mom had realized everything after leaving her body.

Amartya knew that her mom didn't want her to face the same thing and had stayed on till the right time to guide her and was now free to move on and so was she...

The ashram had given her a new life. She had actually not been living till now. She had just been going to the hospital, coming home and then going to the hospital. Life had been just a mere existence, a routine. She hadn't been living her life in the right sense at all. Now here at the ashram, she felt so full of life and energy. She also wanted to learn yoga and *pranayam kriyas* which Swamiji's disciple taught everyone in the early evening. Today, she would start learning yoga and *kriyas*.

Life was going to be secure and meaningful now. She was a soul, she had accepted this and now she wanted to experience all the goodness she could. She was on the path of self-realization and she felt everything was just correct. Amartya loved listening to Swamiji's discourses. The overall peaceful existence of the ashram attracted her. She felt one with nature and one with herself too.

She started getting involved in all the ashram activities. She spoke to everyone at the ashram and contributed as much as she could in the maintenance of the place. She swabbed floors, cleaned vessels, cooked, watered plants and did everything that came on her list of duties. She learned to smile all the time and felt great peace.

She chatted with the cats, dogs and cows at the ashram. She fed grains to the birds. There was so much to learn here. She understood now why young boys like Sivan and Raghu were serving Swamiji and had decided to live a celibate life. They had realized the need to seek self-realization very early in their lives. But she too was not late. She had finally found the inner peace that she had come looking for. She was happy staying at the ashram.

Chapter 29

Amartya ran across the hall, up the stairs. She rushed to her room and sat down on the bed. Tears were flowing from her eyes. Swamiji's words rang in her ears.

"Amartya, my child I know you are very happy here at the ashram. But we must never forget the purpose of our life. I am glad you took to the path of self-realization. You have been able to clear most of your insecurities. But in this journey you have forgotten one important purpose for which you had come here. You have to help Shivani. She needs you. You both are connected due to the karmic accounts of your past lives. Only you can help her and that is the reason you had been feeling a pull towards her. Had I told you this earlier, you wouldn't have believed me. But over the last three months after doing so much *sadhana*, you know now what I mean. You are at peace here and do not feel like going anywhere. But you have left one task half done. Go my child. Go to Kolkata, the girl is waiting for you. Bring her here. We will bring her out of her misery."

How had she forgotten about Shivani? For one moment she felt like she had been so selfish. She recalled sending a leave extension mail two months ago. She had not called Ragini. How was Shivani now? Suddenly the thought of her patient and the sufferings she might be facing made her flinch.

But she realized that unless she herself wouldn't have taken the path of self-realization, how could she ever have helped Shivani? She would have to thank Swamiji for reminding her of her duties. The life at the ashram was so peaceful. She did not feel like going back to the hospital life in Kolkata. What did she want to do? Did she want to practice as a psychologist? What was the purpose of her life? She would have to continue with her *sadhana* at the ashram and find out her goal in life. She would not report to the hospital. She would go to Kolkata and bring Shivani and Ragini here at the ashram. She would resolve the rest of her issues after bringing Shivani to the ashram.

She was feeling better now after taking the decision. She would have to tell Swamiji about it.

She spoke to the disciples at the ashram and arranged for a ticket to Kolkata. She was able to get a ticket for the same night. She would have to call Ragini and find out Shivani's condition.

She would call her up before leaving tonight. She packed her bag and then decided to leave the bag at the ashram. She hadn't completed her journey. She had lots more to learn. She would just carry her handbag. She would go to Kolkata and bring Shivani to the ashram.

Amartya waited as the phone rang at the other end. Had Ragini left Shivani at the hospital and gone back to Mumbai?

"Hello," said Ragini.

'Thank God, Ragini was there with Shivani.' Amartya sighed with relief and said, "Hello, Ragini, Amartya here."

"Doctor! Where have you been? I have been constantly calling the hospital and they had no idea of your whereabouts. Shivani has improved a bit. She still doesn't speak and stares into space. But I feel that she likes to stay in the house and she feels comfortable and secure."

Ragini continued, "Though her eyes are not blank like earlier, she seems to be looking for someone. I was feeling so lost and worried doctor. I was hoping and praying you would call me. Doctor, where are you?"

"I am in Mangalore, Ragini. There is a lot I need to tell you. I came here looking for a solution for Shivani. I knew that the treatment which would be adopted by the hospital would not be correct for her. I wanted an answer and I am here at Swami Shripathi's ashram."

"Doctor, what are you doing in an ashram? I thought..."

Amartya listened to Ragini whose voice had trailed off as though she had lost track of what she had to say.

"Ragini, do you trust me?"

"Yes doctor, I do. When you did not call during the last four months, many a times I felt that you had dropped Shivani's case. But my inner voice assured me that you would never do such a thing. Yes doctor, I trust you and I know whatever you suggest would be the best possible treatment for Shivani."

"Listen Ragini, I will see you tomorrow morning at your house. You book flight tickets for Shivani and yourself for Mangalore. I have a return ticket for tomorrow night's flight. Try to get tickets for the same flight. We will fly to Mangalore and then we will stay at the ashram where Swamiji will guide Shivani and I am sure, she will be perfectly alright in just a few months. In fact, I am sure we will see changes in her in the first week itself."

"Doctor, I have heard a lot about this Swamiji. I know he has great power. I will make the necessary arrangements. See you tomorrow morning. You don't know how glad I am to hear your voice."

Amartya disconnected the phone. Ragini had sounded excited and relieved. She must have been tensed. Obviously, she would have been worried. She had left her husband at Mumbai and was staying in Kolkata with her daughter who was suffering from acute depression. Amartya could almost visualise the stress that Ragini had faced. No doctor, no news at the hospital, a depressed daughter who could react anytime in any manner. Poor Ragini... Amartya was keen to see Shivani. She knew things would change once Shivani was brought to the ashram.

Swamiji had immense positive energy and the ashram was the right place for Shivani's treatment. Amartya knew why Ragini had done what she had done twenty years ago. She understood now that everything was just karma. Everyone encounters happiness or misery based on their karmic account. Ragini had suffered a lot for her mistake.

Amartya called a taxi to go the airport. She wanted to bring Shivani. Her purpose of leaving the ashram was very clear. She would entrust Shivani's responsibility to Swamiji and stay back till Shivani recovered. During that time she could continue on her journey of self-realization.

She boarded the flight and was eager to reach Kolkata. She recalled Swamiji's advice. He was right. She had left Shivani's treatment halfway and embarked on her own journey. But she would set that straight very soon.

***

Amartya rang the bell of the apartment. It was early in the morning. The airport had been very crowded. She found Kolkata a bit overcrowded after seeing Mangalore. She was already missing the peace at the ashram.

Ragini opened the door. Amartya saw tears glistening in Ragini's eyes as she smiled.

"Hello doctor," said Ragini wiping the tears with the back of her hand. Amartya entered the house and saw Shivani seated on the wheelchair staring at the wall. Amartya sensed restlessness in Shivani's eyes. *At least there was some expression in her eyes now*. Ragini's observation had been right. Shivani was probably searching for Amar.

"Doctor, have you informed the hospital? Are you planning to stay back with us at the ashram?" asked Ragini.

Amartya thought for a moment before replying, "I have not informed the hospital and I am not planning to. We will fly to Mangalore tonight. I am not sure about my future plans. I need to stay for a while at the ashram before I decide. Till then I will be sending in leave extensions. They might hold on to the requests for a while. Hopefully, before that I will be able to take the right decision. Ragini, have you informed Mithun about your plans?"

Ragini answered, "I spoke to Mithun two months ago. I told him everything honestly. He was very angry. He just banged the phone and did not attend my calls thereafter. I too stopped calling. I just knew that I was not doing anything wrong."

She continued, "In fact, I was feeling that finally I was doing the right thing. And nothing or no one could stop me from being with my own daughter."

She continued, "And then after a week, he called me. He said he had been thinking about everything. He apologized for his behaviour. He came thrice in the last two months. He felt very sad after seeing Shivani's condition. He has told me to do whatever I can to help Shivani come out of this state. He said he owes this to his friend Amar. He became very sentimental when he saw Shivani for the first time. All his anger and pent-up resentments just melted away. So doctor, now I have full support from Mithun and I have nothing to worry. Shivani is my daughter and I will take care of her all my life or at least till the time she needs me. I have informed him about my visit to the ashram at Mangalore. He was not sure whether it would help. But he said it was better to try everything possible. I was terrified when the hospital informed me that you had applied for long leave. I really had no idea what to do."

"Doctor, honestly if you wouldn't have contacted me for another week, I was planning to take Shivani with me to Mumbai for treatment. Mithun had already spoken to some leading psychiatrists. But somehow I had full faith in you and thankfully you called. I am really very glad to see you. I have this feeling you know. Something inside me... some voice which says that things are going to change for the better. I just hope the feeling turns into reality and my Shivani will become normal again. I want to see how she is as a normal person. And doctor, I spoke to Aparna also yesterday. I told her we are going to Mangalore for treatment. I did not tell her that you are with us. Aparna is a very good girl. She visited us often and she also helped me a lot in settling in with Shivani."

Amartya helped Ragini with the packing and soon they were on their way to the airport. They were stuck in a traffic jam but they managed to reach the airport on time. They finished the check in formalities quickly as the airport staff knew they had a patient on board and special care and attention was provided for Shivani. Soon they were inside the flight.

As they settled in the plane, Amartya looked out of the window. Though she had lived for so long now in Kolkata, she felt a longing to reach Mangalore. The peace and tranquillity of the ashram was like a magnet and she felt drawn to it.

After the flight landed, the cabin crew took over Shivani's responsibility. They wheeled her out of the airport and settled her in a special cab which Amartya had arranged in advance. As the cab sped across the countryside, Amartya breathed in the fresh air. This was where she belonged. This was her home, her mom's home. Ragini was looking out of the window mesmerized by the natural beauty around.

"It is very beautiful but a bit laid back, isn't it?" she asked.

"Yes, the place has its own pace, a peaceful and slow existence which reminds us how stressed and overworked we are in the city. I am sure you will like the ashram. We will be reaching the ashram in a few minutes."

Amartya could almost see the small road which led to the pathway of the ashram. After she had paid off the cab driver, she wheeled Shivani while Ragini managed the bags.

The security saw her coming and rushed out to help her. Amartya smiled and thanked him. Within minutes there were four or five disciples helping Shivani and Amartya knew she had taken the right decision. She felt like seeing Swamiji immediately. She hoped he was free.

After they entered the building, she peeped inside the hall and saw Swamiji sitting and talking with his disciples about the management of the ashram. He saw her and motioned her to come. Amartya had tears in her eyes. She felt like she had come home to her father. She walked up to Swamiji and knelt before him. She bowed and he blessed her.

"Where is Shivani?"

Amartya waved at Ragini who was standing at the entrance of the hall. Ragini wheeled Shivani inside to where Swamiji was sitting.

Amartya knew that Swamiji's positive energy would start flowing and heal Shivani. Swamiji looked at Shivani. Amartya knew he was sending positive energy vibrations to Shivani. Ragini sat down with her hands folded. Amartya sent a silent prayer for Shivani.

"She is going to be alright very soon, Amartya. You help them settle down in a room here on the ground floor. Put Shivani and Ragini in the room adjoining this hall. There will be so much energy flowing, Shivani will have to respond. She will have no choice. The divine grace of the supreme power will bring her out of this misery. We are merely his tools. He will do the work through us."

Amartya knew that Swamiji would be meditating and so motioned to Ragini to help her wheel Shivani out.

Once outside, Sivan came and helped Amartya in settling Ragini and Shivani in their room. Amartya could feel a lot of positive energy in that room.

As if sensing her thoughts Sivan said, "Swamiji used to meditate in this room earlier. Some time back he moved to the room he is in now which is smaller than this one. He said he doesn't need such a big room and preferred a small one. But yesterday he was meditating in this room the whole day. Now I know why he was doing that. Swamiji never does anything without a purpose."

Ragini stared after Sivan as he left the room. "He is so young. Why is he living here at the ashram?"

"He completed his studies and from the time he was a young boy, he was attracted to the ashram and Swamiji, so he came here and has been staying here since then. He says he wants to serve Swamiji and he is very happy with the way he is living his life."

Amartya continued, "Ragini, there are some basic rules at the ashram which we need to follow. Everybody has to do some chores to help in the upkeep of the ashram. Even Swamiji does his share of chores. Also, everyone comes to the main hall for meditation at 3 a.m. in the morning. After that there is chanting of mantras and then we sing *bhajans*. At times there are discourses too. Swamiji speaks great words of wisdom. The stories he tells from the scriptures and of his experiences are worth listening to. It changes our entire perspective of life. We will take Shivani and seat her in the hall from 3 a.m. She will receive lot of positive energy during the meditation and the chanting of mantras will invoke her inner consciousness and I am sure she will start reacting very soon."

Chapter 30

Amartya went upstairs to her room. She realized that she felt like she had come home. Her home in Kolkata did not feel like home anymore. She belonged here. *Or didn't she?* She had to walk further on this journey of self-realization to understand in depth the purpose of her life. She still felt that studying the intricacies of the human mind was something very interesting. But now there was more to learn. She had to understand the deeper depths of the soul. This was more challenging, fascinating and something she wished to do. Studying about the soul in detail would help her understand people better.

If and when she did go back to her career, she would find it easier to deal with her patients. She was not sure whether she wanted to go back to her profession. But the urge to help people and bring them out of their mental traumas and suffering was very strong within her.

She could not lose her focus now. It was important to stay in the present moment. Her career could wait. She had to resolve some of her personal issues. She decided to send positive energy to Gary and forgive him. She had to do the same for her dad too. Her fear and insecurities were almost gone now. She felt safe here at the ashram. But she could not stay here forever.

Amartya felt glad that she was able to focus on her thoughts with so much clarity. Earlier when thoughts on personal issues would pop up, she would just push them down into the deepest recesses of her mind. But now she had the strength to tackle those issues.

She had been too attached to her thoughts and fears. She just had to release them. She knew now what she had to do. Her thoughts drifted to her patient, Shivani.

From tomorrow morning Shivani would also sit in the meditation hall. She knew that Shivani would be affected by the positive energy in the hall and she was sure that her patient would start responding immediately. The room where Shivani was sleeping was the room where Swamiji had meditated for hours on end. The room emitted immense positive energy. She had felt it…

Amartya was sure that Ragini would manage to bring Shivani to the meditation hall at 3 a.m. When she walked into the meditation hall five minutes before 3 a.m., she saw Ragini wheeling Shivani into the hall. Shivani's eyes were closed. She was sleeping.

Amartya gave a mat to Ragini. She sat down on the floor beside Shivani's wheelchair. Everyone had assembled and had started mediation. Amartya took a deep breath and closed her eyes. She hoped that Ragini would also be helped by the immense positive energy in the ashram. Amartya knew that Ragini was also emotionally unstable. After chanting mantras and listening to Swamiji's discourses, there was a definite chance that Ragini would start changing and become emotionally stable.

After the meditation everyone started chanting the mantras. Amartya was glad that Ragini knew most of the mantras and was easily able to join the others. She noticed that Shivani was sitting upright now and staring at Swamiji.

When everyone was chanting, Amartya noticed Shivani's eyes flickering and wandering everywhere in the hall. This was a sign. Something, some emotion had been roused in the girl and she was going to respond. It was a gut feeling…

After the *bhajans* when everyone was dispersing, Amartya asked Ragini,"How was it? Did you feel good? It is good that you know the mantras. I had to learn them."

Ragini who was almost in tears said, "Doctor, it was a beautiful experience. I was not sure what to do during meditation, so I just sat and sent prayers for Shivani. And the chants and *bhajans* were so positive. I am sure my Shivani will be alright now. There is some energy here. Like when we go to a temple, we feel so positive and so strong. I am getting the same feeling, in fact hundred times more. Will Swamiji be giving a discourse now? I would really like to listen to his *satsang*."

Amartya knew what Ragini was feeling. The ashram was such a place. The energy was profound and everyone could feel it. She saw Swamiji walking towards them. Swamiji kept his hand on Shivani's head.

"Bless you my child! Now come out of your trance. You know that it is not leading you anywhere. I will show you the path and lead you to the soul you are seeking. You will have to use this body to experience that. Do you understand that? If you ignore this body, you will never in this lifetime be able to meet the soul you are longing to meet. So don't neglect the body. It is the medium to shed our karmas."

Shivani screamed aloud and started crying. Her body shivered and Amartya knelt down beside the wheelchair to check her pulse and calm her down but stopped when Swamiji motioned her to step back.

Amartya stood leaning against the wall. She was unable to comprehend exactly what Swamiji was trying to do. She saw Ragini standing beside Shivani's wheelchair, looking at Swamiji with her hands folded. Swamiji looked into Shivani's eyes as if he was commanding something. After a while Shivani calmed down and dozed off.

"Take her inside. Put her on the bed and dispose the wheelchair. She will not need it anymore. She will walk and go about doing her things on her own from now on," said Swamiji.

Amartya bowed and wheeled Shivani out of the hall into the adjoining room. The room was very big and had two cots. With the help of some other lady disciples at the ashram, they lifted Shivani onto a cot.

"Ragini, you sit beside Shivani and call me as soon as she awakens. I will be in the kitchen. You can see the kitchen from the window here. I want to be here when she wakes up. I will finish my chores and get back soon."

"Doctor, let me do the chores. You should be here when Shivani wakes up."

Amartya accepted the switch and was sure Ragini could manage easily and get along very well with all the other inmates at the ashram.

She was feeling restless. She sat down on the other cot. She leaned back on the headboard and crossed her legs. She smiled.

She had learnt to sit this way comfortably only after coming to the ashram. She had been used to sitting on chairs, plush sofas and not on the floor and rarely cross-legged. There was a lot of energy in the room. She could feel it. She closed her eyes and decided to focus on her thoughts. She started feeling positive vibrations in her body. After a while she heard, "Where am I? And why am I here?"

Amartya opened her eyes and saw Shivani sitting on the cot looking at her. Amartya got up and sat beside Shivani and said, "Shivani, this is an ashram. I am your doctor, your psychiatrist."

"Why am I here? I don't want to live. I want to die and..." her voice trailed off and she started crying.

Amartya looked at Shivani who was staring at the wall, tears running down her cheeks. She wondered why Shivani had not completed the sentence. She had wanted to die and what? Amartya knew that prodding her now wouldn't be right and so she let the girl be. Instead she asked, "Will you come out with me to the hall outside? We can sit there and talk."

Shivani replied, "I will come out but I will not talk. I will not. I don't want to talk."

Amartya got up and hoped Shivani would follow her out of the room alone, without help. She walked out of the room and after she entered the hall, she turned behind and saw Shivani walking out of the room slowly. Swamiji had been right. The wheelchair was no longer needed.

Swamiji was in the hall speaking to Sivan about some arrangements for the next discourse which was to be held in the ashram grounds. Sivan told her that a festival was coming up and people of the town were eager to listen to Swamiji's discourse.

After Sivan left, she went and sat in front of Swamiji. She turned around and saw Shivani sitting on a chair near the window. She was looking outside. Amartya sighed. Amartya knew that after Swamiji had commanded Shivani's soul to come out of trance, the soul had obeyed and now Shivani was no longer in a trance. *Now how was Swamiji going to bring Shivani out of her misery? How was he going to make her understand that Amar was no more and it was his soul that she had been communicating with?* Amartya had no answers to these questions and with hope in her eyes she looked at Swamiji.

"Amartya, my dear child, stop tormenting yourself. Your duty is over now. You were the medium to bring Shivani here. She will soon be out of her misery. I am also a medium used by the universal power. We are all just actors and playing our parts. We have all come here to finish the role we were sent to play. But we generally do not play our roles well, accumulate karma on the journey and then come back again to clear those karmic debts and then again accumulate some more negative karma and the karmic layers just goes on increasing. On the path of self-realization, we understand that every thought, word and action creates karma. We are under the false impression that it is an action or a word that is counted as karma."

He continued, "Every thought is energy and negative energy created is accounted as negative karma. We are all connected to each other by our karmic debt. There were some debts between you and Shivani from your past life which brought you together."

Swamiji closed his eyes for a few minutes. Amartya sat silently thinking over what he had said. Swamiji was her Guru, her guide. He was her mentor.

Swamiji opened his eyes. He said, "My child, you have brought Shivani to the ashram. It was all destined. You have resolved the issue with her. From now on she will start her journey of self-realization and soon she will have all her answers. But remember that your journey is not yet complete. Some personal issues need to be resolved. But I am sure your *sadhana* and dedication will lead you on the right path."

Amartya understood what Swamiji was saying and knew now that Shivani would be alright. She turned to check Shivani and saw Ragini standing beside her and knew that Ragini had heard all that Swamiji had said.

Ragini came forward to where Swamiji was sitting and bowed her head and said, "Swamiji, I am guilty of many wrongs. Please forgive me."

"Don't seek forgiveness from me. I have no authority to forgive you. Forgiveness, you must seek from the universal power, the Almighty. You must seek forgiveness from the people who you have wronged. And first of all you must forgive yourself."

Amartya wondered if Ragini was going to confess everything to Swamiji.

"But Swamiji, Amar is no more. He was a very good person. I should not have done what I did. Now because of my mistake my daughter is suffering. She suffered for all these years. I can seek forgiveness from Shivani. But how can I apologize to him?" asked Ragini.

Swamiji replied, "Ragini, what is it that you actually want? Are you seeking forgiveness for the mistakes you committed in the past? First you find out what you want. The journey is long and there are no shortcuts in this. You will need to enter into this with a pure consciousness. If you want your daughter to be cured, she will be cured. You don't have to do anything for that. Just pray for her. That will be enough."

Amartya looked at Ragini who sat quietly lost in thoughts. Suddenly, Ragini burst out crying and said, "Swamiji, I don't know what I want. Just that I have been feeling guilty for so many years now. I don't know what to do. I know I have to do something, but I really don't know what it is that I must do. I am a sinner. I shouldn't have left Amar and Shivani. I blame myself for Shivani's condition. How could I have been so lost in my own needs that I totally ignored my child? I was so selfish and immature. I am feeling ashamed of myself. Please show me a way out of this Swamiji, I beg of you."

Swamiji looked at Ragini with compassion and said, "See child, what you did in your past was already destined. It was part of your karmic account. It was not correct. The feeling of guilt and torment you have been facing also was destined. You were trapped in the strong pull of *maya*. Many of us are. Instead of crying and blaming yourself for your daughter's state today, you start thinking positively. Give her all the love you can. But remember that when she starts talking and responding and realizes who you are, she might not accept you. Be prepared for rejection. Love her even then. You have realized your mistake and that is important. Don't waste your energy in regrets. You cannot bring back the past or you cannot change anything from the past. Accept it. You have accepted that you made a mistake and you are repenting now. Forgive yourself, forgive all others concerned."

Swamiji continued, "Child, you have to move on. It was destiny that brought your daughter back to you. It is destiny which has brought both of you here. Amartya and I are just the medium that the Almighty used to bring both mother and daughter back together. I will give you a mantra. You keep on chanting it all the time. Join everyone in the morning for meditation and reflect on yourself at that time. In a short time you will get all your answers. Do not worry. Once you forgive yourself, Amar will also forgive you. I am sure if you truly love Shivani, she too will forgive you. The Almighty is very kind. You will see that everything is alright and all of you are happy. Just chant the mantra I have given you with full devotion and love."

Amartya knew that Swamiji was speaking to Ragini and yet she felt like whatever he was saying was applicable to her too. She touched Swamiji's feet and went and stood beside Shivani. Shivani was looking out of the window. Ragini came and stood beside her. Amartya knew that Shivani would soon start talking and behaving like a normal person. After that it would be easier to explain about Amar's soul communicating with her. Probably, Swamiji had something else in mind. Amartya had no idea what he had decided about Shivani.

Shivani just sat there near the window not willing to get up. She sat there as though she had not heard anything. Amartya looked at Swamiji hoping to get an answer. He just motioned her to leave along with Ragini.

Amartya looked at Ragini and with her eyes made a sign to leave the hall.

"What about Shivani?" Ragini asked in a low voice.

"What about me? Why are you so concerned? Who are you anyway and why have you come back? Do you think that if you come now and say you are my mother, I am going to believe it? I am not a fool. You cannot be my mother. She ran away with some other man. What proof do I have that you are my mother? In case you are truly my mother, why did you leave your second husband and come to me now? Have you come back hoping to stay with dad and me again? By the way, dad is no more. He died soon after you left. I am alone, have been alone and don't need anyone. Especially you," shouted Shivani.

Amartya stood rooted to the spot listening to Shivani accusing Ragini. So Shivani had listened to each and every word that had been spoken. Ragini's confession, Swamiji's explanation, everything...

Swamiji got up and walked up to Shivani who after her outburst was staring out of the window. Tears were flowing from her eyes. Amartya's eyes were glistening with tears too. She looked at Ragini who was sobbing loudly and muttering, "I knew it, I knew it..."

Swamiji kept his hand on Shivani's head and said, "Now that you have come out of your trance, you are getting emotional. You lack stability and I don't blame you. The circumstances in your life have made you unstable. But you are a lovely being. Just do not utter anything negative and if possible chant the mantra that I will give you now. It is a special mantra which will give you a lot of peace and soon you will see the person who you are longing to see."

Shivani was trapped by Swamiji's words. His words had the magic. No one could say no to him. Also he had mentioned that she could see the person she was longing to see.

The thought of being able to see her guardian angel brought about an instant change in Shivani who said, "Swamiji, I will do what you say. I have to see him."

And then pointing her finger towards Ragini she said, "I do not want to say anything ill about anyone but I do not want to stay here with that woman."

Swamiji in his soft voice told Shivani, "If you want to stay alone, I will tell someone to arrange a room for you or if Dr. Amartya is willing, she can move in with you and Ragini can occupy Amartya's room."

"I don't mind staying with anyone except that woman." Shivani blurted out.

Amartya gave a nod accepting the switch in rooms. She turned and saw Ragini sobbing quietly and wiping her tears with the tail end of the white sari she was wearing.

"Don't cry Ragini, didn't Swamiji say that you need to give unconditional love to your daughter. Just be at peace and have patience. Pray and chant the mantra. Things will work out. You have to trust Swamiji." Amartya tried consoling Ragini who had become very emotional.

"Yes doctor, you are right. I just couldn't control my emotions. I... I don't know but... anyway what you are saying is right. I will move up to your room, and involve myself in the chores at the ashram. I want to serve Swamiji. He is a great man. He has made my daughter speak. I am sure soon she will be alright and back to her normal self. What more could I have asked for?"

Ragini wiped her wet cheeks with the back of her hand and continued, "It is very selfish and mean on my part to stand here and cry instead of rejoicing that my daughter has come out of her trance. I owe this to Swamiji. I can never thank him enough. He is my God. I have to thank you also for taking the effort to bring us here. I will pray with full faith and devotion for Shivani."

Amartya watched as Ragini touched Swamiji's feet and walked out of the hall. Shivani was staring out of the window again. Her eyes were still glistening with tears.

Chapter 31

Amartya climbed the stairs to go to her room. She would pick up her things and move to Shivani's room. When she reached upstairs she saw that Ragini had already done the packing for her. She was glad to see Ragini smiling.

"Doctor, I have already packed your things. I am feeling better now. I felt bad when Shivani said all those things. But I deserved it. I have done a grave wrong and I am here to rectify it. I am going to correct all my mistakes and will not leave the ashram till I have done that."

Amartya thanked Ragini and as she climbed down the stairs with the bag in her hand, she wondered what power had made Ragini leave her daughter and go away. But then her dad had also left her and her mom. Gary had left her too. What was it that people were seeking? Was it love or insecurity which made people commit such grave mistakes in life? Or was everything destined?

She still had to find answers to so many questions. Swamiji would answer them for her but in his own time. He never told everything at once. But then that was the right way. If he told her ten things at once, she would never understand.

***

Life was back to routine at the ashram. Amartya went for the group meditation at 3 a.m. Shivani did not join her in the first week. Ragini came in exactly on time everyday. She had started liking Ragini. She observed that Ragini was very hard working, as she did a lot of work at the ashram. She never missed any of the discourses and joined her for the yoga exercises and *pranayam* in the evening. Amartya saw small changes in Shivani after a week.

One night Shivani said, "Doctor, could you wake me up at 3 a.m. tomorrow? I want to join you all for group meditation. I am ready to do anything to meet him. He has to come to meet me. I will call him when I meditate. I will also chant the mantra that Swamiji has given me."

Amartya nodded and speculated as to how much of her depression did Shivani remember.

"Shivani, you know that I am your doctor, right?"

"Yes doctor, I know. I heard everything that you spoke that day to Swamiji."

So the girl had actually no memory of things before she came out of her trance. She just remembered that 'he' had left her and she wanted to see 'him' and after she came out of her trance, she had heard everything spoken between Swamiji, Ragini and herself and assumed most of the things. It was better to leave things as they were. There was no point in telling Shivani now that Ragini had come months ago and had been taking care of her. All that would come to light in due course.

"I will wake you up from tomorrow. It is good that you have been chanting the mantra given by Swamiji. All your wishes will soon be fulfilled."

Amartya knew that once Shivani joined everyone in the meditation hall, she would receive vibrations of positive energy in abundance and that would release her insecurities and fears.

The same evening after completing their yoga, Ragini said, "I want to speak to you, doctor. It is personal. I wanted to speak to Swamiji, but I thought I will speak to you first. Can we talk now?"

Amartya replied, "Surely we can talk now. Tell me what is it that is troubling you?"

Amartya sat on the stone steps of the ashram building. Ragini came and sat beside her. She said, "Doctor, I don't know how to tell you. But yesterday when I was seeking forgiveness from Amar,

I think I saw him. No, actually, I heard a voice. I was so confused. I was scared and it was late in the night and I didn't want to disturb you. I heard Amar. I am sure it was him. He told me that he has forgiven me and that he was happy that I was taking care of Shivani. He then told me that he had been with Shivani until lately till she had got engaged. But now he can't come as he has moved on in his journey to take another body. He said he would try to see Shivani one last time if possible."

Ragini sighed and sat quietly for a few minutes lost in thoughts.

"Doctor, was this just a dream? An illusion? Or was it real? How is it possible? I am not even sure I should tell Swamiji about it. I mean Amar died so many years ago. How could he have appeared before Shivani? Now he has moved on and says he cannot come. I find this whole thing so unbelievable and yet I want to believe it. It is only when I believe that I can find solace. If Amar has forgiven me, I can be at peace. I know my daughter will also forgive me. My life will be peaceful and without regrets after that. Shall I tell Swamiji about it?"

"Ragini, what you saw was not an illusion. It was real. It was Amar's soul communicating with you. You have to listen to Swamiji's *satsang*. I have heard him speak about the soul and its journey. I will try to tell you whatever I have understood from Swamiji's *satsangs* so far."

Amartya continued, "The soul never dies. It just takes different bodies. Just like we shed clothes, when the soul feels it has completed its duties in a particular body or feels that this body will not help in releasing the accumulated karmic debts, it leaves the body to take another form. Amar's soul left the body sooner than expected and so lingered on knowing that he had some unfulfilled duties and only when he saw his daughter secure and happy with Arun, he decided to move on in his journey of life and death."

"When we say soul, it is not a ghost or some form. It is just energy. We are all energy bodies. We are actually just energy. When we say a soul talks, it is not the verbal sound that connects us to a person. It is the energy vibration. So when souls communicate there is an energy exchange. Do not feel confused or doubt what you hear or see. Just trust yourself and have full faith in Swamiji."

Ragini asked, "But how is that possible? It is so difficult to believe all this."

Amartya could understand how Ragini was feeling. She said, "See Ragini, Swamiji has complete knowledge on all this and has achieved the knowledge after severe penance for years and years. Many scientists and doctors come and meet Swamiji asking for explanations to some supernatural occurrences. You heard Amar's soul. His energy vibration connected with yours and you both communicated. Just believe it. What you hear from others or read about is always a belief and whatever you experience is the ultimate truth. I am glad that he has forgiven you. You can move on now. Shivani will also forgive you. I am sure about that. The mantra chanting is a very powerful process. It invokes the cosmic energy in the universe and results in lot of vibrations and changes in our life. It releases a lot of your negative karmic baggage. Just go on doing whatever you are doing and everything will be alright."

"Thank you so much doctor. You are truly a saviour. You have understood the intricacies of Swamiji's teachings so well. Probably, very soon you too could start preaching. The way you explained everything to me was so good, I have no fears now. I will tell Swamiji about my experience tomorrow after the *bhajans*."

Amartya was glad that Ragini was treading successfully on her path of self-realization. Amar had forgiven Ragini. It was time for her to forgive Gary and her dad. She had been avoiding that for a while now. Unless she did that she would not be able to move on in her journey. So what was holding her back? Why was she so reluctant to forgive Gary or her dad? She had to do that immediately. She had to settle the past issues before she decided on the path she wanted to take in her career.

Swamiji had said rightly that there was no shortcut or easy path to self-realization. It was a lot of hard work. Very few people would be ready to take so much effort. Every soul would want to seek self enlightenment and be one with the universal consciousness. But *maya* would override this desire and the soul would either not start on the path of self-realization or leave it halfway through.

She walked inside her room and saw Shivani sitting in deep concentration chanting the mantra under her breath. Amartya immediately decided to meditate and send positive energy to Gary and her dad. She would forgive them. She would not delay it anymore. She had to move on. It was as though seeing Shivani and listening to Ragini had charged her up to resolve her issues.

Amartya sat cross-legged on her cot, kept a pillow to support her back, closed her eyes and focused on her thoughts.

Her mom had forgiven him. Now she too would forgive him. Wherever he was, however he was, it didn't matter. Swamiji had said that even if the person is no more, the soul will receive the energy. She decided to send positive energy to her dad and forgive him for leaving them. She realized now that he had just played his part. If her mom had suffered, it was because she had been destined to. Her karmic debts had brought about the suffering and he had been the medium. Maybe he also suffered after that. She too had suffered the insecurity of not having a father. But now she was secure. She needed no one, not even Gary. He had gone away from her life because that too had been destined. Her connection with Gary had been brief. Their soul journey had finished and he had left her. His life was probably with some other woman. She did not want to hold on to the resentment and bitterness that she had stored for Gary. No one was worth it. The deep-rooted sadness and suffering she had been feeling would result in negative karma for her. She did not want that. She decided to release all the negative emotions. This would take time, but soon she would be free of all the negative thoughts stored deep down inside her. Then the path would be clear. What was it that she wanted in life? This question was troubling her but she was sure once she cleared her past regrets, she would see her path clearly.

Amartya opened her eyes. She saw Shivani's body shaking. She got up and just before she reached Shivani, the tremors stopped. Shivani opened her eyes.

"Are you okay, Shivani?"

"Yes doctor. I heard his voice now. I, he ..."

She started crying. Amartya held Shivani in her arms till she stopped crying. After what seemed like fifteen minutes or more Shivani said, "I don't believe it. He said he was my dad. How is that possible? I heard his voice. It was 'him' – my guardian angel. Then he said that he can't come now. When I asked him why he was hiding from me and making me suffer, he said that he couldn't come because he was in soul consciousness and was in the process of taking another body. I don't believe this nonsense. What soul and all? It was an illusion, I am sure. Did you hear him? He was speaking so loudly."

Amartya decided not to reply and instead ask Shivani to talk to Swamiji. She knew that he would guide her in the right manner.

"Shivani, why don't you talk to Swamiji about all this? He will tell you exactly what it is that you saw."

"Yes doctor, you are right. I will speak to him tomorrow morning. Now I am afraid to sleep. What if he comes again?"

"Shivani, you wanted him to come, right? Now what happened? Why don't you want him to come?"

"Doctor, he is not coming. That is the problem. I don't want to hear a voice. I don't like it. It is all unbelievable."

"You go to sleep, don't worry. He won't come if you don't want him to. Anyway, I am here with you. You need not fear. Not here at the ashram. With Swamiji near us nothing or no one can harm us. We need to have faith and trust in the universal power."

Amartya waited till Shivani slept off and then went to her cot to lie down. She was feeling tired today. It had been a long day. There had been too many emotional outbursts in just one day.

Ragini had heard Amar and now Shivani. Amar had moved on... That was good.

How would Swamiji convince Shivani that it was Amar who she had been seeing and that now it was Amar's voice she had heard? And even if Shivani believed Swamiji, how would she react? The girl was very sensitive and unstable. Amartya was worried about Shivani. But Swamiji had said that her duty as far as Shivani was concerned was over. So why was she simply worrying about the matter. Swamiji would resolve Shivani's problem. She just hoped Swamiji would give a discourse which would help Shivani to get all the answers she sought.

Chapter 32

Amartya got up at 2.30 a.m. and after taking bath decided to wake up Shivani.

Amartya tried waking Shivani but the girl was very sleepy and so she let her be. She decided to come back after the meditation and see if Shivani was awake. Amartya entered the meditation hall and just as she had hoped, Swamiji informed everyone that he would be giving a discourse after the mantra chants. Amartya knew Swamiji would be able to clear everyone's doubts. He was a sea of knowledge. She felt gratitude for him.

She saw Ragini standing near the window. She walked up to her and saw tears glistening in her eyes. It was ten minutes to three and the meditation hall was half full. Amartya asked, "Ragini, why are you crying? What happened?"

Ragini spoke in a low voice, "I just want Shivani to accept me. I had convinced myself that Shivani is happy with Amar and so it did not hurt me much. But since I have learnt of her past, Amar's demise, her hostel life and everything, I feel responsible for Shivani's struggle. I feel so guilty now for having gone away. How selfish I was! Just because I felt Amar doesn't love me like before and Mithun showered a lot of love, I left my daughter and went away. I regretted my decision after a few months but I couldn't think of coming back. The divorce papers had been signed. I am unable to remove the guilt from my mind."

Ragini covered her face with her palms and with a shiver in her voice she continued, "Now that I have got my daughter back, I want to take care of her, be with her and give her lot of love and security. I want to atone for my sins. But she refuses and doesn't want me to come near her. Tell me doctor, what to do?"

Amartya knew that there was no time to discuss all this and so just said, "You meditate and chant the mantras. Somehow I have a feeling that today Swamiji's discourse will give us our answers. He knows everything. We need not even tell him our doubt or problem. He just knows and so he will speak something today which will clear each person's doubts. Each of us is here with a purpose. We all have our own doubts and questions. We will surely find the way today. He will show us the way. I am sure."

Amartya took a mat and sat down to meditate. Today she would end her inner turmoil with Gary.

Gary was a nice guy. He had truly loved her. Then why had he gone and had a relationship with some other woman? Had he been fed up with her? No. It had never seemed like that. Why? The question revolved in her mind. Today she would connect to the cosmic universal energy, the Almighty, and she would receive her answer. Amartya started chanting the scared word "OM" in her mind. After a while she started getting her answers.

Gary had always loved her. He would neither have left her nor had an extra marital affair if she hadn't created the thought in her mind. But she did not remember creating the negative thought. Probably, in her subconscious mind she had created the thought that Gary would cheat her.

Her dad had left her mom and so she had felt that men were unstable. That emotion had stayed and she had created unwanted negative energies which had eventually driven Gary away from her. When she had told her mom about Gary, she had reacted negatively. She had been sure that Gary would cheat her or leave her. She had created that energy. Amartya too had accepted her energy subconsciously and Gary had done exactly what they both had feared he would. The fact that any man who would have married her would have left her was clear now. On the conscious level, she had been very practical and confident that Gary would not cheat her the way her dad did. She had convinced herself that Gary was different. But she had created a lot of negative energy and it had turned Gary away from her. Though what Gary had done was wrong, he was not to blame. He had acted as the medium to make her experience what she had been destined to experience. She had created everything. No one was to blame. It was just something that had to happen. And her mom had gone away because she was destined to live only till that time.

So now if Gary had nothing to do with her mom's demise, shouldn't she forgive him totally? Amartya knew it was time to change her perspective about Gary. She had always doubted him though not consciously, and felt that he would in due course cheat her. Finally, on seeing the woman in their house with Gary, she had reacted unreasonably. She hadn't waited to listen to Gary's explanation and had immediately filed for a divorce. It was as though she had been taking revenge with her dad for having left her mom.

She had mixed up two different stories. But now she did not feel any regret. Even if she would have continued her marriage with Gary, she would never have trusted him and the marriage would have ended in a disaster. Thankfully, she had not conceived. So it was only she who had suffered. But that was all over and in the past.

Now what was it that she wanted in life? She had to analyze her options and move on. Did she want to become a disciple and serve Swamiji all her life? Did she want to take Swamiji's blessings and go back to America? Did she want to marry again? The questions started flooding and she wanted a respite.

Thankfully, the chanting of mantras began and she joined everyone religiously. She loved to chant the mantras as the words created a very positive vibration. Amartya wanted answers for her questions.

Just before Swamiji started his discourse, Amartya decided to go and bring Shivani. As she reached the door, she saw Shivani walking towards the hall.

Some other members of the ashram who did not stay at the ashram had come too. Probably, they had been informed by the others about the special discourse today.

Swamiji began, "Today there seems to be quite a crowd. All of you are here hoping to ask some questions and receive answers from me. But I know all your questions already!"

Everyone in the room laughed. They were all relieved that soon they would have all the answers and their doubts would be cleared.

Swamiji continued, "Okay, today I will speak on birth and life after death. Let me ask you all a few questions first. Why do you think we take birth again and again? What is this cycle of life and death? To understand that first we all need to know, accept and remind ourselves that we are the soul and not the body. The body is just a garment we are wearing. Each birth we will be wearing a different garment and to identify each body we give names. So what happens after we die?"

"I know that you all know that we take birth again as a different person. We are born again but in another form, a new life. So, why do we die? We die because our karma fixes our destiny and decides how long we would live in one particular body. So, does the karmic account end with the body? No, it does not. The soul leaves the body carrying along with it the karmic account and enters another body. During the time the soul takes to enter another body, the soul thinks about its past deeds in its past lives. It can see everything clearly as it is in pure soul consciousness form. The soul is in a transition period and looks for another body, another form. The choice of the next birth is based on the accumulated karma. Now karma is what we think, say or do. It can be negative or positive. Based on our past karma we are born again. In the next birth, we carry forward all our pending karma, both good and bad. So there is only one soul but it takes various forms and many lives. Each life the soul vows to attain enlightenment and join the eternal soul, the Almighty, the universal consciousness. But the soul forgets its promise as soon as it enters a body. When it enters the body, it forgets its promise and gets pulled by *maya* and starts collecting good and bad karma."

"Now when a soul leaves the body, it always stays back for a while to see what it has left behind and when it sees half done jobs or responsibilities, it lingers on hoping to help the survivors. Many a times this is not possible. But sometimes, the soul manages to transfer energy and communicate with another soul who is in a body. This is mistaken as ghosts or spirits by some people. Souls, when not in a body are just energy. It is just like we are the soul, the energy, but in a body. Verbal speeches, actions are all possible when we have this body. Energy cannot be destroyed. Souls take some time before they enter another body. Soul years are slow unlike ours. Souls can communicate with each other whether in a body or not."

"We actually do not need words and actions to communicate. Our souls can communicate with each other. But it is not acceptable in the human world and so all this knowledge was not discussed and a fear was linked to the existence of the soul."

"The soul is pure energy when it first starts its journey. That is, when the first time it enters a body. But during the journey it accumulates good and bad karma and then unable to release the negative karma in that life, it takes birth again. This cycle goes on till the time the soul reaches self enlightenment."

"This happens very rarely as most of us are caught in the cycle of life and death due to *maya* which entangles us in various ways. We find it very difficult to understand that we are in the grip of *maya* and we suffer. These sufferings lead to more karma."

Swamiji paused. He looked thoroughly at the crowd and after a few minutes resumed his talk.

He said, "Don't worry. It is not all that depressing as it sounds. We experience a lot of things in each life, both good and bad. Bur from now on remember that whatever you experience, you account it to yourself and do not blame other souls. Never blame anyone else for what is happening in your life. You are responsible for each and everything that is happening in your life. The people who you think are hurting you or making you happy are just a medium who have come to give you the experience you sought. Just accept each and every person the way they are and perform good karma with a positive outlook. Each life you get is precious because you get the opportunity to attain enlightenment. But we are all so lost in our karmic debts that we just live, die and are born again to die again. It is when we lift our hand to blame others for our misery that we create lots of negative karma."

"Stop and understand that whatever you are suffering or enjoying today is just the result of your past actions done either in this life or your past lives. Live a simple life, help others, love all the other souls, accept responsibility for all that is happening in your life and you will feel deep happiness." With this Swamiji blessed everyone and ended the discourse.

Chapter 33

Everyone in the hall was mesmerized by Swamiji's words. Amartya knew that each one had understood the discourse in their way. She realized that the answers she was seeking were right there within her. She just needed to ask herself. She knew now that each soul knows deep within what is right or wrong. She had known too. But she had never listened to her inner voice. After a while, the inner voice had stopped talking to her. But it was still there. She just needed to ask and her inner voice would answer and it would know the right answers to all her questions. It was the same for everyone.

She saw Shivani walking towards her. Was Shivani going to tell Swamiji about her experience?

She turned to see if Swamiji was free. Swamiji motioned her to come near him. Ragini got up at the same time and walked along with her to the other end of the hall where Swamiji was seated. Most of the people were dispersing and Swamiji waited till all of them had gone before asking Shivani, "Did you have any questions?"

Shivani replied, "Yes, Swamiji. Yesterday I heard his voice. But he told me that he was my dad. How can that be? My dad died in an accident. This person used to come and speak to me. I used to see him. One day he just disappeared and now I can hear his voice and it is the same voice. So why can't he come now? And how can he be my dad? I don't even remember dad's face. But I remember how this man looks. He was my guardian angel and he is no longer there for me." Shivani started sobbing.

Swamiji replied, "Shivani, child, you are a soul. Now you are in this body and your name is Shivani. Your dad died all of a sudden, unexpectedly and when he saw his body lying there at the accident scene, he stayed on. He did not want to leave you alone. He was always around you, guarding you. Your twenty years are just twenty days for a soul. When you started feeling lonely and felt the need for an elder, he started talking to you and you gave him the form. He was never a physical form. Now if you tell me that you did not remember his face, it is true in a sense that your conscious mind did not have any memory of your father's image. But your subconscious mind had stored an image of your parents. So when you heard your dad's voice, you automatically gave him a form and that form was the same that you had stored in your intra-cellular memory. It was your dad who you used to see all these years. When he saw you were stable, comfortable and happy with your fiance, he decided to move on in his journey. Let him go Shivani. Don't hold on to him. He has to continue his journey. You have to understand that. If you don't let him go, he will suffer in his next birth. In his new birth, he will not even know the reason for his suffering. You have your own life to live. He was there as long as you needed him and now your mother is also there with you. Go and live your life happily. You do not have to feel so insecure. Your dad's blessings will always be with you."

Amartya saw Shivani's eyes brimming with tears. Shivani started crying uncontrollably. It was like she had released a dam of pent-up emotions. Swamiji sat with his eyes closed.

After a few minutes, tears still flowing down her cheeks she said, "How can I accept her? She left me and went away with some other man. Dad must have felt so bad. And then dad left me too. I felt so lonely. I was alone..."

Shivani didn't complete her sentence and continued sobbing. Ragini crumbled down on her knees with her head bowed down, tears running down her cheeks. Amartya left them to resolve their personal issues and went and stood by the window staring outside. She could hear Swamiji speaking.

Swamiji continued, "Shivani, learn to forgive. Whatever you faced in your life was part of your karma. Ragini just behaved as per her karma. She knew that she had committed a grave mistake. She has been regretting it for all these years. Also she never knew that Amar had left his body. She always had the image of father and daughter living happily in Kolkata. She suffered as she never conceived again. The loss of a daughter left her aggrieved. She is seeking forgiveness and it is for you to grant it now and release both of you from your karmas. Accept your mother. A mother is one who brings you in this world. She never chose you. Remember it is the soul who chooses its parents. You chose Amar and Ragini as your parents because of your past karma. This is what you wanted to experience in this life and you have been experiencing exactly what your karma dictated. It was your destiny. Now it is in your destiny to get back the love of your mother. Do not refuse that."

Amartya decided to sit beside Shivani who was crying incessantly. Ragini knelt down in front of Swamiji.

"I do not know how to thank you, Swamiji. You have released me from a lot of grief. Today I am feeling very light."

Swamiji smiled and said, "You have to thank Dr. Amartya for bringing you here. Though she was just a medium to bring both mother and daughter together, she has done her job in a very positive manner. She lost her mother and she knows the emotion of bringing a mother and daughter together."

Amartya smiled at Ragini who thanked her profusely for uniting her with Shivani.

Shivani looked at Ragini with a new light in her eyes. Amartya could sense that both mother and daughter would bond together now. Suddenly, Ragini rushed out of the hall. She came back in a couple of minutes. She held the photo album in her hand. She opened it and started showing Shivani the photos one by one. Shivani turned the leaves of the album checking each photo minutely. She smiled. Ragini whispered something to Shivani and they both started talking in a low voice totally unaware of their surroundings. It was as though they had never parted.

Amartya looked at them totally amazed. She wondered if Shivani would speak to Arun and clear his doubts. But then that would be entirely Shivani's choice. She had her mother now with her. They both would together decide her course of life. Maybe Shivani would go to Mumbai with her mother. There Ragini might look for a nice handsome boy for Shivani to marry. They had innumerable options to choose from. As long as they were together, nothing would go wrong now.

Amartya bowed to Swamiji and left the hall.

She went and sat down in the garden outside. The trees were swaying in the cool breeze. She caressed the goose bumps on her body and shivered. It was very cold. It was going to rain. She looked up at the clouds. The sun was hidden beneath dark clouds. The grass was trimmed to perfection and she moved her hands over it. The green grass felt soft to touch.

She did not want to go back to America. She did not want to marry again. She did not want to go to Kolkata and join Carewell or any other hospital there. She did not want to stay at the ashram and live the life of an ascetic.

The grass was damp. Raindrops on the grass glistened in the sunlight. She looked up to see the sun which was partly visible now. The dark clouds were accumulating with fury. She touched the drops of rain which had fallen on the grass.

She would start a centre in Mangalore. A centre to help mentally ill patients and people with psychological problems... She had some money saved which she could use for leasing a small place for the centre. Later on she could expand depending on the income she earned. She would also start a free Spiritual Healing program at the centre. Yes! Swamiji would inaugurate the centre. She would name the centre after her mother.

She had taken this birth to help people. That was the purpose of her life. She had always been interested in the complexities of the mind and now she would research on the complexities of the soul, philosophy of karma and the journey of a soul.

She got up and started walking towards the ashram building. She wanted to tell Swamiji about her plans. She would tell him that she had received all the answers.

The raindrops fell heavily. She walked slowly enjoying the rain lashing on her. She held her palms together to collect the water but it just slipped from between her fingers. She lifted her face to the sky wanting the rain to drench her completely. Her face was wet with rain and the tears which were flowing from her eyes...she could see her path clearly.